"Don't just stand there, Miss Bruc...

Purdey stood frozen as Jared Faulkner went on, "Come in—I have something I want to say to you."

Her first instinct was to turn and run, but as she took a half step backward, Jared strode quickly across to her, catching her wrist and pulling her into the room. Then he closed the door and leaned against it, a mocking smile twisting his lips.

"So—we meet again," he said meaningfully.

Purdey stared at him, feeling sick inside. "What—what do you want?" she managed to ask.

"Why...to renew an old acquaintance. What else?"

His voice was silky, but she sensed an undercurrent of anger. His voice became suddenly savage as he added, "Confidence tricksters like yourself ought to realize that the people they defrauded will want revenge."

SALLY WENTWORTH began her publishing career at a Fleet Street newspaper in London, where she thrived in the hectic atmosphere. After her marriage, she and her husband moved to rural Hertfordshire, where Sally had been raised. Although she worked for the publisher of a group of magazines, the day soon came when her own writing claimed her energy and time.

Books by Sally Wentworth

HARLEQUIN PRESENTS

HARLEQUIN ROMANCE

Don't miss any of our special offers. Write to us at the following address for information on our newest releases.

Harlequin Reader Service
901 Fuhrmann Blvd., P.O. Box 1397, Buffalo, NY 14240
Canadian address: P.O. Box 603,
Fort Erie, Ont. L2A 5X3

SALLY WENTWORTH

echoes of the past

Harlequin Books

TORONTO • NEW YORK • LONDON
AMSTERDAM • PARIS • SYDNEY • HAMBURG
STOCKHOLM • ATHENS • TOKYO • MILAN

Harlequin Presents first edition October 1990
ISBN 0-373-11309-9

Original hardcover edition published in 1989
by Mills & Boon Limited

Printed in U.S.A.

CHAPTER ONE

'PLACE your bets, ladies and gentlemen. *Faites vos jeux.*' The croupiers' unemotional voices, grown tired now, sounded through the elegant main room of the gambling club even though it was gone three in the morning. Perdita Bruce lifted heavy eyelids and forced herself to smile at the four players who still sat at her semicircular blackjack table. All except Alex, of course; for him, the smile was genuine. He was still playing, but it was only to pass the time until he could take her home; Purdey could tell from the desultory way he picked up his cards. She turned over her own cards and added them up. Seventeen. 'Pay eighteens up,' she intoned. Three of the players, including Alex, grinned, but the other gave a dissatisfied grunt and heaved himself up from his chair. He threw a couple of low-value chips on the table as a tip for her and ambled heavily away. Purdey thanked him politely and put the chips in the pool that would be divided among all the croupiers by the management.

'Ignorant oaf,' Alex murmured to her behind his hand.

'Sh.' She puckered her lips to hush him, but he chose to believe that she was blowing him a kiss and blew one back, which made Purdey both frown and grin at the same time. It was impossible to be serious or annoyed with Alex, he was such a charming, fun-loving character. At the moment he was in love with her, but he was only twenty-one so she didn't think for a moment that it would last. He was confident that it would though, of course, and was so besotted that he kept asking her to marry him. But Purdey, at nineteen, had seen far more of the world than he had, and refused to commit herself. Though she had to admit that she was enjoying his attentions. It was fun to go around with him, and she appreciated the meals he bought her, as she had to save every penny she could. But most of all she was grateful to him for taking her home from the club in the early hours of the morning when otherwise she would have had to take a taxi. That she also had to fight Alex off every time went without saying, but he took it all in good part and, if anything, grew more in love with her. But Purdey had few illusions and knew that she was capable of handling Alex—and of letting him down lightly if he got too serious.

There was a stir by the door as the man who had been playing at her table went out and some latecomers came in. They were a small party of six people, three women and three men, all in evening dress and looking as if they'd been to a nightclub. Purdey gave a hidden sigh and hoped they were keen roulette players. Alex glanced across too, and forgot to pick up the card she dealt him.

'Good lord!' he exclaimed. 'It's Jared.' Purdey raised her eyebrows at him and he said, 'My uncle.' He gestured with his head towards the group that had just come in. 'The tallest of the three men.'

Purdey looked across, but the man he had indicated was just turning away to speak to one of the women in the group. She saw that he was certainly tall, at least six feet two, and correspondingly broad-shouldered in his well-cut jacket.

'I wonder what he's doing here,' Alex muttered with a slight frown.

'Come to play roulette, presumably,' Purdey returned as she saw the group go over to one of the other tables. 'Why else would he be here?'

Alex pulled a comical face. 'Mother always sends for him when she thinks I need telling off or some fatherly advice.'

Purdey laughed and counted her cards. 'Nineteen. A stand-off, madam,' she said addressing a woman player whose cards added up to the same number. 'Will you stand or change?' She finished the deal, passed over a number of chips and the woman and her escort moved away, leaving Purdey and Alex free to talk. 'Your uncle doesn't look old enough to be a father-figure,' she remarked, glancing across at the roulette table.

'He isn't. That's the trouble. Actually, he's only about ten years older then me, much younger than my father was. Jared is my mother's brother, you see. But since father died she's got in the habit of depending on him. And she thinks that he'll understand me.'

'And does he?'

Alex grinned. 'I'm afraid he does, unfortunately. Most of the time, anyway. But he's pretty good, really. At least he doesn't talk down to me all the time.'

With a small smile Purdey picked up the discarded cards, wishing that the only problem she had was the fear of a ticking off from a protective uncle. Her heart sank a little at the thought of the enormity of her own problem, especially since it seemed to be a losing battle, no matter how hard she and her mother worked. Glancing up, she caught the floor manager's eyes on them, but she knew that she wouldn't get told off for talking to Alex. Because Alex was Alexander, Lord Nash, a Viscount already and the heir to his grandfather who was a very rich man indeed. There was no way the management were going to offend someone who would one day have such a large fortune that he might care to gamble with in their club. So his association with Purdey was more than tolerated, it was tacitly encouraged. With the result that Alex, ever since he had come here with a group of university friends to celebrate sitting his final exams and had immediately fallen for her, spent most of his evenings sitting at her blackjack table like a faithful dog.

'What would you like to do tomorrow?' Alex asked. 'Tell you what, there's a rugby match on at Twickenham.'

Tomorrow was Sunday and the only day Purdey had off from the gaming club, so it was very precious to her. She tried to make it a rule then to have at least a few hours in which to rest and recuperate, a period in which to recharge her mental and physical batteries for the coming week, preferably in the open air. Quite often she didn't even manage that, because there were domestic chores to do and Toby to visit at his special school. And a rugby match? Purdey could think of a hundred things she'd rather do with her few hours of leisure. But it would be out in the open and Alex was always good fun to be with. So she teased him a little, pretending to think about it, but when he started to look anxious she relented and agreed to go.

'Great,' Alex enthused. 'We'll go out to lunch and then straight on to the match.'

'OK, but I have to be home by seven,' Purdey cautioned. 'No meeting up with some of your friends and going on to a party the way you did last time.'

'Ah, but you know you enjoyed it,' Alex protested with one of his boyish grins.

'I said it had been an education,' Purdey corrected. 'All those rugby songs—I'd never heard anything like them! You're a corrupting influence, Alex Nash.'

He pretended to look hang-dog and bent forward to lean his forehead against hers. 'But you still love me though, don't you?' he cajoled.

'Who is the corrupting influence?'

A harsh voice broke through Alex's words and they both swung round, Purdey in surprise and Alex in rueful expectation. 'Hello, Jared,' he acknowledged.

His uncle had come across to the blackjack table without them noticing and now stood, dark and austere, beside Alex. He seemed even taller close to, and his face was as lean and hard as his body. A lot of men came to the gaming club, of all different types, and over the months that she had been working there Purdey had gradually got to place them into categories. There was the expansive type of man who was everybody's friend, a little loud, and who came to also enjoy the social side; then there were the rich men of many nationalities who came only to gamble, lured there by an addiction that they couldn't resist. Some of the most frequent visitors were the newly rich yuppies, venturing into this sort of atmosphere and finding it a heady enjoyment, and against them were men like Alex, whose families had owned land and money for so long that they had never known what it was like to be without it, but who still loved to gamble. But, of whatever type, they were all of them drawn to the gambling tables and fell prey to the excitement of the possibility of winning. All except for a very few men who stood out from the crowd: men who were immune from the temptation of the green baize tables, who could play to win or lose without letting their emotions become involved, men who were in complete control of themselves and knew it. And Purdey had come to find that there was some indefinable air about such men that was instantly recognisable. Perhaps it was something self-contained, something of withdrawal in their manner. Perhaps it was the slight amusement in their eyes as they surveyed their fellow men, as if they were the only adults at a children's party; they thought it infantile but were willing to be indulgent.

Purdey looked at Alex's uncle and knew instantly that he was one of the few, but what puzzled her was the swift glance he gave her, a glance that lasted only a second but made her feel as if he had seen everything there was to see and found nothing to hold his attention.

'Alex.' His uncle nodded in return. 'I haven't seen you for some time. Is this where you've been hiding yourself?'

'Hardly hiding,' Alex protested. 'And just what are you doing here, Jared? This isn't your scene. Has Mother been to see you?' he asked suspiciously.

Jared's slightly arched eyebrows rose. 'Does she have cause?'

Alex immediately looked discomfited, like a boy caught out in some mischief and not knowing what to say. But he jumped from being ten to being twenty-one magnificently, drawing himself up and saying, 'Not on my account, no.' Then he turned to Purdey and said, 'Purdey, may I introduce my uncle, Jared Faulkner. Jared, this is Purdey—Purdey Bruce.'

'Miss Bruce.' The reply was very formal, his nod the briefest, and Purdey was almost sure she saw a momentary flash of contempt in his cold grey eyes. But, whether there had been or not, she knew instinctively that Jared Faulkner had disliked her on sight.

'Mr Faulkner,' she returned with equally chilly formality and no nod at all.

The grey eyes settled on her for a moment, but his expression was completely unreadable. So unlike Alex's, Purdey thought with a shiver, and turned to smile at the younger man. He grinned back at her, oblivious to the sudden coolness in the atmosphere. 'You haven't told me what you're doing here yet,' he reminded Jared.

'A dinner party at the Hindmarshes' became extremely boring. A group of us went on to a night-club, and then someone suggested coming here.' He indicated the party he was with with a wave of his hand.

'Oh heavens, yes. My mother dragged me to dinner there once. He insisted on talking about his experiences in the Diplomatic Service all evening. But Mother always goes at least once a year because she was at school with his wife or something, and feels sorry for her.'

They talked on for a few moments about common acquaintances, shutting Purdey out. And it had been done deliberately, she was quite sure of that. Jared Faulkner had taken one look at her and then treated her as the rich treated their servants, like a piece of furniture. And because she was on duty at the table she had to just stand there, growing angrier but unable to walk away.

'I've got a couple of tickets for the match at Twickers tomorrow,' Jared remarked. 'How about coming along?'

'Sorry, I can't,' Alex answered, turning to Purdey with a grin. 'I've already managed to persuade Purdey to go with me.' And he audaciously reached out to take hold of her hand.

Normally, she would have pulled away at once, telling him the management didn't allow that sort of thing when she was on duty, but his uncle had put her back up so she smiled at Alex, one of her special smiles that lit her face, and said, 'I wouldn't miss it for the world.'

Alex gazed at her in besotted enthralment and kissed her hand. Purdey continued to smile at him, but out of the corner of her eyes saw Jared Faulkner give a quick frown of annoyance and flick another contemptuous glance her way. But he said easily, 'Perhaps I'll see you there, then. Goodnight, Alex.' Alex murmured a response without looking round and Jared said curtly, 'Miss Bruce.'

Purdey turned slowly and made no attempt to hide the mockery in her eyes, mockery that said quite plainly that she had the power to shut him out just as he had shut her. 'Goodnight, Uncle Jared,' she said tauntingly as she turned back to Alex, and hid a smile of satisfaction at the sudden blaze of anger in Jared Faulkner's eyes.

The manager came over shortly afterwards and told her that she could go home. Purdey left the club by the back way that led into a side alley. Alex was waiting for her just outside, eager to protect her from any danger. They kissed for a little while but it was cold, a wind blowing from the north that lifted the rubbish that had accumulated in the alley and sent it whirling into the air. Alex turned up the collar of his thick camel overcoat and Purdey thrust her bare hands into the pockets of her padded anorak that was becoming shabby with constant wear; the club gave her an allowance to spend on the dresses she wore while she was working, but it didn't extend to a decent coat.

'Come on, let's get to the car.' Alex put his arm round her waist and they ran out into the main road and along to his little Italian sports job. They got in, but had to wait for the windscreen to clear of frost before they could pull away. From here Purdey could see the entrance to the club, and as they waited she saw Jared Faulkner and his party come out and go over to a beautiful Rolls parked just outside. He unlocked the doors and saw the women in, smiling down at one of them in particular as he did so. His wife, presumably. Purdey gave a shudder as she imagined what it must be like to be married to someone as cold as that. But maybe he wasn't cold all the time. She turned to Alex to ask him more about his uncle, but he had turned on the radio and it was a new record by one of their favourite groups, so she listened instead and as they discussed it afterwards she forgot all about Jared Faulkner.

At that time of night it took only a quarter of an hour to drive to the flat in Islington which Purdey shared with three other girls. Alex had learnt by now that she would never ask him in, but he reached for her eagerly and kissed her goodnight with as much avid passion as anyone could show when in a small two-seater car and hampered by gear lever and handbrake. Purdey returned his kisses happily enough; she liked Alex and she liked his kisses. OK, he tried to go too far at times, but she knew how to hold him off, and he was such a well brought up person that he would never force himself on her. So they always parted friends, even though Alex would have liked them to be so much more.

'Alex, I must go.'

'Must you? Can't you stay here a bit longer?'

'*No.* If I don't go in now, I'll be too tired to go out with you tomorrow.'

That threat made him reluctantly draw away, and he got out of the car and came with her to her front door, waiting until he'd seen her climb the three flights of ill-lit stairs and go into her flat before he left. Purdey closed the door quietly and crept into the bathroom to undress and remove all the make-up she wore to look glamorous at the club, making as little noise as possible so that she didn't wake the other girls—not that they showed as much consideration for her when they got up in the mornings. Going into the bedroom, Purdey groped her way in the dark to a chair and dropped her things on to it, then gratefully slid between the cold sheets of the single bed, trying to stop her teeth chattering, afraid of waking Diana who slept in the other bed.

The room felt even more cold then usual, and Purdey couldn't get warm. She counted the blankets and found that there were only two. Damn! Diana had pinched one again. Getting out of bed, Purdey tried to take the blanket back, but found Diana had wrapped it round herself, so instead she put her anorak over the covers and huddled into a ball to try and keep warm.

But sleep wouldn't come and her mind drifted. She thought of Alex and then of his uncle. She was willing to bet that *he* wasn't shivering in a cold bed tonight! She thought resentfully of his Rolls-Royce and the gold watch and cuff-links that he'd been wearing. But then a picture of his face filled her mind. It had been such a strong face, hard and with high cheekbones, his eyes slightly hooded, adding to that closed, contained look. There had been mothing at all soft about him, even his lips had had a slightly cynical twist, and Purdey was quite sure that he would make an implacable enemy. She shivered again and turned over. Heavens her feet were freezing. It was no good, she'd have to lash out on a pair of bed socks or a hot-water bottle. Preferably both. She toyed covetously with the idea of an electric blanket, but knew that she couldn't afford the extra electricity, let alone have enough to buy one. No, it would have to be a very thick pair of socks and perhaps a hot-water bottle if she could get one from Oxfam or one of the other charity shops. Not until Toby's operation was paid for would there be any money for luxuries like electric blankets.

At the thought of Toby, Purdey smiled despite the cold. He was such a happy little boy, even though he had so many problems. And he was so young, only eight. It just wasn't fair! But then, when was life ever fair? Purdey thought with a cynicism that was too old for her years. Toby was Purdey's brother. He had been born prematurely as the result of a car accident in which their father had been killed and their mother injured. For several months it had been touch and go whether he would live, but he had clung on to life tenaciously and eventually been allowed home. But without their father life had been a struggle, and then had come the bitter news that Toby had something wrong with his eyes and was going blind. After much heart-searching, Helen Bruce had allowed her son to go away to a special school so that he could learn how to cope with his blindness, feeling that he especially needed it as he was an extremely intelligent child with the promise of a bright future ahead of him but for this.

The money to pay for the school had come from the insurance claim after the accident, but Mrs Bruce had gone out to work too, while Purdey had done well at school and gone on to college to take a course in economics and business management. She had been at the college only for a term though, when they had been told by a specialist that there was now a new operation that could be performed that might save Toby's sight. But the technique wasn't available in England. Toby would have to go to America to have a preliminary operation, and if that was successful to return a few months later for the second part of the operation. He would also need someone to go with him to take care of him.

At first Purdey and her mother had been overwhelmed with joy at the news, but soon realised that they would have to find all the money themselves. Thirty-five thousand pounds. A great deal of money by anyone's standards, and a fortune by theirs. They had no house to sell and nothing to borrow against. They had left the area where they had lived most of their lives and taken a flat near Toby's school, so it would be difficult to try to launch a local appeal for help. Mrs Bruce had tried to get help from various charities, but there were many people who wanted the operation and they could only promise her a small sum towards it. 'Never mind,' she said grimly. 'I'll raise it somehow.'

'*We'll* raise it,' Purdey corrected. 'I'll give up college and take a job.'

'You will not!' her mother declared forcefully. 'I'm not having your future ruined. You'll stay on at college but you can take a Saturday job and work in the holidays. That will be a tremendous help.'

They had talked it over and begun to save, but soon realised it would take them years, while the cost of the operation was increasing all the time. In despair Helen Bruce had taken a live-in job at a hotel, while Purdey had gone to share the flat in London. That way they could give up their own flat and put the rent money towards the trip to America. Purdey had got a Saturday job, and although the pay was fair it wasn't enough. Someone at the college had told her about the vacancy for a croupier at the gambling club and she had gone along. It meant working until the early hours six nights a week, but the money was extremely good and there were tips as well. It made studying for college very difficult, but there was always the lunch hour and weekends to try to catch up in. Sleeping was difficult too, but Purdey had got into the pattern of sleeping for only a few hours at night and again for a couple of hours in the evenings before she went to the club. It was hard, it was terribly hard, but Purdey only had to think of Toby being able to see again and she found the strength to go on.

The following day was still cold, but bright and sunny. Purdey dragged herself out of bed in time to get ready to meet Alex, and was waiting for him on the pavement when he drove up. She always waited for him there. The flat was squalid, but the best she could expect for the rent she paid. Purdey had to put up with it, but she didn't intend to inflict it on her friends as well. Especially Alex, who was the only bright thing in her life at the moment.

He had once asked her why she lived so far out—which was a tactful way of asking why on earth she lived in such a terrible place, but she had merely said that she had to. She hadn't told him about Toby; it was her problem and, like the flat, she didn't intend to inflict it on anyone else. Besides that, she didn't want pity. And Alex was so kind and generous; Purdey knew that if she told him he would immediately offer to give her some money which she wouldn't be able to take, not even as a loan. How could she go on holding Alex at arm's length when she owed him money, for heaven's sake? No, it would make things just too awkward and complicated to be beholden to him. And anyway, Alex wasn't that well-off himself. He had fantastic expectations, but at the moment he lived on the allowance his mother doled out to him while he decided what he wanted to do career-wise. But perhaps the final argument against it was the thought of the number of years it would take Purdey to pay him back; her heart sank at the thought of being in debt to someone indefinitely like that.

He arrived early, as he always did, eager to be with her again, and hooting happily when he saw her so that everyone turned round to look. He hugged her when she got in the car, and she laughed and told him he looked like a bear in his thick coat and long scarf. He made her feel young and happy and carefree, feelings that she'd sometimes thought she'd lost completely before she met him. And that happiness lasted all through lunch and on to the rugby match. But at half-time they went into the bar to have a drink against the cold, and they ran into Jared Faulkner again.

Purdey was standing at the back of the bar, letting Alex fight his way through the crush of equally determined men, and saw the two meet and speak. They got the drinks and pushed their way out again, Jared coming over with him. Today Purdey was wearing hardly any make-up and she had drawn her long ash-blonde hair into a thick pigtail instead of the loose, glamorous style she used for the club, so when Jared looked round for her, his glance swept over her at first. Then he did a double-take and came back, his eyes narrowing as he looked her over and took in her jeans and anorak.

'Here we are. I didn't spill a drop,' Alex said triumphantly as he handed her a glass of beer.

'Thanks.' Purdey smiled at him and let him put his arm round her possessively.

'You remember Jared; I introduced you to him last night.'

'Yes, I remember,' Purdey answered tightly, and lifted her eyes to be met by his uncle's cool appraisal. There was something in his face that surprised her; last night he had been contemptuous, but now there was a frown between his brows as he looked at her, almost as if he was studying her, summing her up all over again. 'Good afternoon, Mr Faulkner,' she greeted him.

'Miss Bruce.' If anything, his voice was even colder.

Alex made a gesture of protest that nearly spilt his beer. 'You two are so formal. I know he's a million years older than you, Purdey, but Jared's really quite human when you get to know him. You mustn't be afraid of him.'

Her chin tilting, Purdey said clearly, 'I'm not afraid of him.'

Jared's eyes were still on her and a distinctly challenging glint came into them at that remark, but Alex was still speaking and he turned to listen to him.

'And you mustn't intimidate Purdey, Jared. You must be very nice to her because you're going to see a great deal more of her in the future.'

'Am I, indeed?' His brow rose questioningly.

'Yes, because I'm crazy about her,' Alex said proudly, and leaned forward to kiss her on the tip of her nose.

In any other circumstances Purdey would have wrinkled it at him and made some remark that would have been suitably deflating, but she was aware that Alex's open demonstrations of his feelings annoyed Jared, and so she perversely smiled at Alex instead, which pleased him and made him give her a soulful look.

'If you'll excuse me,' Jared said coldly. 'I'll see you some other time, Alex.'

'Going already?' Alex dragged his eyes away from Purdey to look at Jared in surprise.

'Yes. I think with any luck I might find some less cloying company elsewhere.' And he turned and walked away.

'What on earth did he mean by that?' Alex exclaimed. 'Sometimes I can't make Jared out.'

'Can't you?' Purdey watched his tall frame until he

went outside. 'You know, I have the feeling that he doesn't like me very much.'

Alex looked at her in astonishment, unable to believe that anyone could dislike the girl he was so mad about. 'Of course he does. It's just that he takes time to get to know people and relax with them.'

'He seems so cold,' she said with a remembered shiver.

'Oh, he's OK, really,' Alex assured her, speaking with all the casualness of a favoured nephew. 'Although I must admit he doesn't suffer fools gladly. But he's always around if you get into trouble and need help. I can talk to him about things I wouldn't dream of telling my mother.'

Purdey wondered fleetingly whether he'd told his mother about her, but pushed the thought aside; as she wasn't serious about him, she had no particular wish to meet his family. 'What does Jared do?' she asked instead.

'He's the head of the family bank.' And when Purdey goggled at him Alex laughed and added, 'It's only a merchant bank. But he has other directorships in the city, too.'

'Isn't he rather young for that?'

'No, not Jared,' Alex said in genuine admiration. 'He always knew where he was going and wasted no time in getting there.'

'A whiz-kid?' Purdey hazarded.

Alex laughed. 'I can't somehow see Jared describing himself as that.'

Purdey grimaced. 'No, perhaps you're right. How about his wife—do you get on with her?'

After drinking down the last of his beer, Alex shook his head. 'Can't—he isn't married.'

'Wasn't that his wife he was with last night?'

'No. Told you, he's a confirmed bachelor. That was probably his latest girlfriend.'

'Does he have many?'

'Quite a few, I think, over the years. Some have been real lookers, too. I remember one girl he went out with; I used to fantasise about her for months.' Purdey punched him in the ribs and he laughed and threw up his hands. 'I surrender. She wasn't a patch on you, though,' he said loyally. 'You're the most beautiful woman I've ever known.'

'Why didn't he marry any of them?' Purdey persisted, ignoring his too-fulsome compliment.

Alex sighed. 'I don't know. Because he never fell in love with one of them, I suppose. He hasn't been lucky. Purdey, look, you know I'm . . .'

'Does he have affairs with them?' she interrupted.

'What? Oh, you're still on about Jared. Well, yes, of course he does. Purdey, will you please listen to me?'

She realised that another proposal was coming up, but saw that he was determined and looked at him obediently. 'OK, I'm all ears. But if you're going to ask me to marry you again, then the answer's still the same.'

'But we're both a month older than when you said we were too young,' he protested.

Purdey laughed at him, but then took pity on his woebegone expression and leaned forward to kiss him. 'Tell you what,' she offered. 'If you're still in love with me in four years' time, I'll marry you on your twenty-fifth birthday. How about that?'

'Four years? That's a lifetime.' Then he grinned. 'But at least you've promised to marry me. I'm not going to let you get out of that. From now on I'm going to consider us engaged.'

'Oh, Alex, you're incorrigible. Come on, the teams are coming back on the field. Let's go and watch.'

Purdey hadn't taken Alex at all seriously, but it seemed that he was because he started speaking of her as his fiancée, even in the club. She tried to put a stop to it in a playful way, but he wouldn't listen, and she realised after a couple of weeks that she would really have to do something about Alex. Although she didn't want to; she liked him too much and didn't want to hurt him. And she was going to miss having him around, but he had to be made to realise that she wasn't in love with him. Sunday was coming round and Alex had promised to take her out, although he'd got all mysterious about it and wouldn't say where, so Purdey made up her mind to tell him then, letting him down as gently as she could. But on Saturday evening the matter was taken completely out of her hands.

She had been working on a college project up until the last minute, and was in the bathroom applying the heavy make-up for the club when there was a ring on the doorbell. Darn! It was eight o'clock and the other girls had already gone out, so she would have to answer it, although it was probably only a neighbour who wanted some change for the gas meter. Grabbing up an old towelling robe. Purdey put it on over her underwear and went to answer the door. The bell rang again under an impatient finger before she reached it, and she pulled the door open in some annoyance.

'OK, I'm coming as fast as I can. I . . .' Her voice trailed off and her eyes opened wide in startled surprise as she saw that the caller was Jared Faulkner.

'Good evening.' His eyes ran over her and Purdey

automatically put up a hand to draw the robe closer together. 'I'm sorry to disturb you, but I wish to speak to you.'

'Has something happened to Alex?' she demanded fearfully, unable to think of any other reason for his coming to see her.

'No. He's perfectly all right. Perhaps I could come in so that we could talk?'

'No.' The reply was instinctive, not only because of the shabbiness of the flat, but also because she didn't want to be alone with a man like Jared Faulkner.

Perhaps he guessed her thoughts, because his mouth twisted into a sneer and he said in a voice like dripping ice, 'I assure you, you have nothing to fear.'

The way he said it, as if she was less than nothing, brought Purdey's chin up defiantly. 'What do you want?' she demanded.

'To talk to you—inside.' And he pushed past her and walked into the flat. The door opened straight into what the girls ironically called their sitting-room. A very small room cluttered with a sofa, table and chairs, and all their belongings they couldn't cram into the even smaller bedrooms, so it was always untidy, always had clothes hanging from the picture rails and dumped on the ironing-board, which never got put away. There were piles of books and papers on the table and on the floor, and underwear drying on a guard in front of the gas fire. It was cold, untidy, and smelly from the meal the girls had shared earlier. Purdey could guess exactly how it appeared to Jared Faulkner as his eyes swept disdainfully round.

'Do come in,' she said sarcastically, her anger fired by embarrassment.

He threw her a scornful look, pulled the door out of her hand and closed it.

Purdey glared at his high-handedness. 'Why have you come here?'

'To tell you to keep away from Alex.'

'What?' She stared at him in open-mouthed astonishment. 'Why on earth should I?'

'Because he's too damn good for one of your type,' Jared said bluntly.

For a moment Purdey was too angry to speak, but then she said in a tight, dangerous voice, 'And just what do you consider my type to be, Mr Faulkner?'

His dark eyes flicked over her contemptuously. 'You're a gold-digger. A cheap little slut who's seen an opportunity to fool an inexperienced boy into marriage so that she can get her dirty hands on his money.'

'How dare you speak to me like that?' Bright spots of furious anger rose in Purdey's cheeks. 'You don't even know me.'

'I don't have to,' Jared retorted. 'Your intentions are perfectly obvious. And there's really no point in putting on the innocent act—I'm not a gullible boy to fall for your tricks.'

'No,' she flashed back, 'you're the type of person who thinks they have the right to burst into someone's home and insult them.' She had the satisfaction of seeing his brows flicker at that, but she went on insultingly, 'And I am, of course, terribly sorry to disappoint you, but I do *not* intend to stop seeing Alex just because a snob like you thinks I'm beneath him.'

'Oh, but you will—because I'm not leaving here until you agree,' Jared answered menacingly.

Purdey stared at him for a moment, chest heaving, the angry flush still in her cheeks. 'Get out,' she said shortly, and went to open the door, but Jared put out his hand and held it shut.

'Not until I get what I came for.'

'Well, you're wasting your time. Not only am I not prepared to give Alex up, but you'll never persuade him to give me up!'

'Oh, but I think he will, especially when he realises you're merely playing hard to get with him, and that in reality you're any man's for the taking.'

'Why, you——' Purdey stepped towards him, her hand raised to strike back, but Jared caught her wrist easily and bent her arm behind her, making her wince. For a moment he glared down at her, enjoying her helplessness, then he bent his head and took her mouth, crushing her body under his so that she couldn't escape.

Purdey struggled wildly, trying to hit him, but off balance as she was she was entirely at his mercy. Except that he showed her no mercy, his lips taking hers with fierce anger, forcing them to open and ignoring her wild curses. With a whimper of helpless rage, she had to stop struggling and hold on to his arm to stop herself from falling at his feet. And it was then, as she grew still, that his kiss got to her. She felt a flame of excitement deep inside her start to grow, licking through her veins, making her senses reel until she felt as if she was drowning, the world swirling around her until only the touch of his lips was real, the only thing left that mattered. She gave a soft moan of discovery and her arm slid round his neck. Jared let go of her wrist and held her closer, pressing her hips against his. Purdey gasped and kissed him in passionate response, her body on fire with this aching need she had never experienced before.

But suddenly he stepped away and she staggered, her legs too weak to support her. He caught her and she stared up at him, unable to believe that this had happened to her. Jared's breathing was unsteady and his eyes glittered down at her. 'So now we both know what you are, don't we?' he said thickly.

'What?' She tried to understand, tried to get her wits back. 'No. I—I never felt like that before.'

He laughed then, a harsh sound that jarred her senses. 'What a fool you are. Do you really think I'm going to fall for something like that?' Lifting his free hand, he pushed aside her robe and began to caress her breasts. 'No, you're just a sexy little cat who can't resist this—from me or any man.' His hand slid inside the thin material of her bra-slip as he fondled her, his fingers knowing exactly what to do to send that flame shooting back through her veins like an erupting tide of heat that consumed all reason. He smiled coldly while he did it, knowing that she couldn't resist, knowing that each second was a further degradation.

Purdey stared into his eyes, like an animal that was too fascinated by danger to run away. She tried desperately to fight the desire surging through her body, to tear herself away from his touch that made her body quiver with erotic sensuality. Because this was wrong, all wrong. From somewhere she found her voice and managed to say unsteadily, 'Take your hand off me.'

His brows rose scornfully. 'But you know you love it.'

'Let me go.' Purdey managed to drag herself away out of his reach. But it was his victory, she knew that; he had chosen to let her go.

With trembling hands she tied her robe tightly about her, but the gesture only made him laugh again. Then he looked at her face and suddenly became angry. 'So—do I have your promise to keep away from Alex?'

'No!' The answer was very positive, and born out of hurt and humiliation.

'Very well, if you won't do so of your own accord, then I shall have to force you.'

'You can't. Alex is crazy about me and I . . .'

'Oh, I know that. But I shall merely remove your opportunity to go on seducing him. I've already spoken to the manager of the gaming club.' He paused to let that sink in. 'You've been fired. You no longer have a job there.'

Purdey stared at him in horror. 'But they can't fire me! I don't believe you.'

He shrugged his broad shoulders. 'Then phone them up and ask.'

'But I've done nothing to make them fire me. I . . .' Her voice trailed off as she saw the malicious triumph in his eyes. 'You swine. I *needed* that job.'

'I'm sure you did.' Again his eyes swept round the room. 'Even a slut like you has to live. So, I'm prepared to compensate you.'

She shook her head helplessly. 'I don't understand.'

'It's quite simple. I'm willing to pay you two thousand pounds not to see Alex again.'

There was a short, shattering silence in the room as Purdey gazed at him in shocked disbelief. 'You—you're offering to pay me money to give up Alex?'

'That's what I said,' he answered impassively, as calmly as if buying someone off was something he did every day.

An intense, cold rage slowly filled Purdey's brain. So cold that it made her forget the emotional turmoil that his kiss had thrown her into, made her remember instead only the toil of the last months and the work that lay ahead, for years probably, for both her mother and herself. And this man thought that she could be bought off. Because he was loaded himself, he thought that all who were less well-off had a price. Her head came up. 'Go to hell!' she said roundly, and meant it.

His eyebrow rose cynically. 'I shouldn't be in too much of a hurry to turn it down. Alex might quite well give you up in disgust when I tell him how avidly you responded to my—advances.'

'And he might well never speak to you again when I tell him how you came here and forced yourself on me,' Purdey countered, too full of hatred to care what she said.

His mouth tightened and Jared glared at her. 'You think you're sitting pretty, don't you? Persuading him to get engaged and to take you to meet his mother tomorrow. Hasn't it occurred to you that one day Alex is going to come to his senses and realise he isn't in love with you?'

Purdey knew that full well, but it was a surprise to find that Alex intended to introduce her to his mother. She was indebted to Jared for that piece of information. It gave her the impetus to say, 'Perhaps, but not before we're married. And you can't stop us from getting married,' she added triumphantly, 'because

Alex is over twenty-one, let alone eighteen. He's his own master.'

Jared glared at her angrily and took a step towards her, but then stopped and balled his hands into fists. 'All right,' he grated. 'How much do you want?'

She looked at him for a moment, then turned away and went to the window. It was snowing and very cold outside; almost as cold as this anger and hatred that filled her brain. Deep in her conscience a small voice told her that she ought to stop this and tell him that she had no intention of marrying Alex, but he had insulted and belittled her once too often for that. Let him be humiliated now. Turning to face him, Purdey said the first figure that came into her head, a sum that was engraved on her brain. 'I want thirty-five thousand pounds,' she said boldly.

It was Jared's turn to stare, and then laugh incredulously. 'You must be out of your mind.'

'Take it or leave it,' she said calmly, enjoying the moment.

'You put a very high price on your . . .' his eyes went over her, his lip curling disdainfully as he mentally stripped her '. . . your very obvious charms.'

Cool now because she had the upper hand, Purdey said, 'Alex is his grandfather's heir, and his grandfather is extremely rich. And they're both lords. Perhaps I fancy myself as a lady.'

'You couldn't be a lady in a million years,' Jared said in sneering insult.

'Careful, if you talk like that you merely push my price up,' she mocked.

'And just how do you justify your price?'

'Alex is in love with me; he'll come after me, which

means that I'll have to find somewhere else to live. And you've made me lose my job, so I'll have to have something to live on until I find another,' she improvised quickly.

'But why thirty-five thousand?'

'Mind your own damn business!'

She shot the words at him, and for a moment he looked completely taken aback. 'Damn *you*, you cheap little . . . No, but you're not so cheap, are you? Not with the price you've put on that beautiful body of yours.'

Purdey strode to the door. 'That was your last insult. On second thoughts, I think I'll marry Alex after all. Now get out,' she said fiercely, and yanked open the door.

His eyes blazed at her, and she didn't think she'd ever seen anyone so furious. 'All right,' he said through gritted teeth. 'I'll pay you your money.'

'When?'

'Now.'

She laughed derisively. 'I don't take credit cards.'

'You won't have to. I'll go to my bank and get it now—in cash. In the meantime, you can pack your things and get ready to leave.' And he abruptly turned on his heel and strode away, running down the flights of stairs as if he couldn't get away quick enough.

Purdey stared after him, then leaned against the doorjamb feeling suddenly weak. Slowly reality began to dawn. Dear heaven, she had actually agreed to give up Alex for thirty-five thousand pounds. She'd sold herself. Well, no, not quite that, but she'd allowed herself to be bought off. She went quickly back inside, realising that she would have to tell Jared the truth when he came back. And a nice fool she'd look! Going into her own room, Purdey sat on the bed and tried to think. Obviously Alex's mother and family were worried about his involvement with her. To them she was just someone from a gaming club, and they probably blamed Purdey for making Alex spend all his time and money there, although nothing on earth would keep him away at the moment when he was so crazy about her. But as she had no intention of marrying him it was hardly fair on Alex's family to go on with her friendship with him. Although she would miss him, and who knew, if he had stayed in love with her until he was twenty-five, she might have got so used to having him around that she might have let him talk her into marrying him, after all.

But Purdey suddenly knew that she would never do that. Tonight had taught her that, if nothing else. When Alex kissed her it had been nice, but nothing more. But Jared's one kiss had opened up a whole new world that she hadn't known existed, and somehow she knew she could never settle for less. So what was the point of staying around here with Alex getting more difficult to handle? Better to split now and get it over. It was going to be difficult enough now that Jared had got her fired from the club, anyway. Her suitcases doubled as drawers, and Purdey quickly packed them. She put on jeans and sweaters against the cold, and wrote a note for her flatmates, enclosing her share of the rent.

She'd just finished when there was a sharp ring on the bell. Surely Jared couldn't be back already? But he was, with a briefcase in his hand.

'Look,' Purdey began awkwardly. 'I was wrong.

I want . . .'

'Oh, no,' Jared said with a snarl as he pushed past her. 'Don't try putting up the price. You've got what you asked for, and you're not worth a penny of that. Here.' He dropped the briefcase on to the table and opened it, displaying the neat wads of notes inside.

Purdey stared, realising what the money meant. Toby would be able to have his operation. Now—not in years in the future. It meant that her mother wouldn't have to live in that terrible, impersonal hotel, working from morning till night. And it meant that Purdey could go to college without having to work every night as well. She'd be able to live with her mother and be able to sleep a whole night through again. And all because Jared was willing to pay her not to marry a man she didn't want to marry anyway.

Suddenly it seemed terribly funny and she began to laugh hysterically.

'Shut up! Stop it. Damn you, you beautiful little bitch, will you stop it?' And he took hold of her shoulders and shook her.

Purdey stopped laughing abruptly and glared up at him, the cold hatred filling her mind again.

'Sign this,' Jared ordered, and took a paper from his pocket.

'What is it?'

'An undertaking that you won't see Alex again.'

Slowly she read it and found that it was also a receipt for the money. Again the appalling reality of what she was doing hit her. 'Oh, but I can't. I don't really . . .'

'Damn you, *sign* it.' Jared thrust a pen into her hand. 'And do it quickly. The very sight of you sickens me.'

Purdey's face tightened as she looked into his eyes, smouldering with anger and contempt. Without giving herself time to reconsider, she took the pen and signed her name.

'Aren't you going to count it?' he asked sneeringly. She shook her head. No, I . . . No.'

'All right. Now let's go. I've got a taxi waiting outside for you.' He picked up her cases and opened the door. Bemused, Purdey picked up her jacket and bag and went to follow him. His lip curled as Jared said, 'Don't forget your blackmail money. You'll need it until the next dupe comes along,' he reminded her derisively.

Slowly Purdey went over to the table. It wasn't too late, she could still back out of this. But Jared needed to be paid back for all his insults. Then the thought came to her; why not take the money and pay it back when she could? If Jared could get it that easily then he obviously wouldn't miss it, but if she returned it then her honour would be satisfied too. Everyone would be happy, in fact. Quickly now, she closed the case, picked it up and turned to him, her head high and her conscience momentarily appeased. 'Right, I'm ready to go.'

CHAPTER TWO

'AH, MISS BRUCE, how are you settling in? Let's see, you must have been with us over two months now.'

'Yes, that's right,' Purdey smiled at Bernard Forster, the director in charge of recruitment for the Tudor Rose Hotel Group. 'I'm enjoying my job very much. I spent most of the first few weeks travelling around all the hotels in the group, so I haven't been in the office very often.'

'But you're starting to get down to a feasibility study on promoting the conference facilities, I understand?'

'Yes, that seems to be the most suitable growth area to start on.'

'And is the office we've given you OK? Do you have everything you need?'

'Yes, it's fine, thank you. And everyone has been very helpful.'

'Good—well, let me know if you have any problems. I believe you're presenting your preliminary findings at the full directors' meeting tomorrow, aren't you?' And, when Purdey nodded, 'Fine, I'll look forward to hearing it.'

He walked on down the corridor and Purdey went to her own office. She was loving this new job. After getting a good degree, she had spent two years working for a company in the north of England, where she had gained the experience she needed to apply for and get her present post. A job she had wanted very badly, not only because it represented a much bigger challenge and a corresponding rise in salary, but it also meant that she would be able to live in the south again and be within travelling distance of the flat where her mother and Toby were living in London. But perhaps the biggest attraction, one that she'd fallen for straight away, was the beautiful surroundings, because the group had their headquarters in a perfect small Georgian house set amid landscaped gardens. The house was actually the dower house of a large mansion and its estate that the group had bought and turned into its first and most prodigious hotel, and one of the directors had had the brilliant idea of making the dower house into the group's head office. After living in the centre of the industrial north for two years, it was marvellous to look out of her window and see green lawns and trees instead of the endless streets and traffic-congested roads. To breathe untainted air instead of diluted carbon monoxide.

Purdey went to the window now and looked out on this sunny May afternoon at trees bursting into leaf and buds coming alive with colour. She smiled, feeling very happy, but then turned to sit at her desk and go over her initial report yet again. She wanted to have everything exactly right for the meeting tomorrow, because she would in a way be on trial. The men who had picked her from the long list of applicants would need to have their confidence in her confirmed, and the directors she hadn't met when she came for her interview for the post would need to be reassured that their co-directors had made the right choice. So she must be sure that she had all her facts absolutely right, and that she'd gone into every aspect; she didn't want to be caught out on a question she couldn't answer.

For the next couple of hours she worked with intense concentration, only looking up when the secretary she shared with two other executives came in to say goodnight. 'I'll tell the receptionist you're working on, shall I?'

'Thanks, Sue; if you wouldn't mind.'

'Much to do?' Sue asked sympathetically.

'No, not really. Just double-checking everything, that's all. I shouldn't be too long now.'

Sue left to go home to her family in the nearby town. At first when Purdey had left college it had seemed strange to have older people working under her and taking her orders, but now she was used to it and had developed a friendly manner, but one that didn't allow advantage to be taken of her youth. She was twenty-three now, and felt quite mature enough to take on this kind of junior executive position.

As she had nowhere to live in the area, Purdey had been given a room in the nearby mansion hotel while she was at the office, but most of the last weeks had been spent living out of a suitcase as she went from one hotel to another. She had quite enjoyed this, and one of the reasons she'd been given the job was because she had no family ties and was willing to travel, but now that she realised what the job entailed she was beginning to feel that she needed some kind of base, although she hadn't had the time to start looking yet. In the meantime, the hotel was fine; they had given her a luxurious although small room, and she

was also given free board. As Purdey was no great
shakes as a cook, that was even better. Today,
especially, it was a big advantage because it meant that
she could work late and just stroll through the lovely
grounds over to the hotel and have a meal served to
her when she was ready.

It was gone seven when she finally left, saying
goodnight to the caretaker and walking slowly
through the grounds over to the hotel. She loved this
part of the day and preferred to take the walk alone.
People were fine, but there was a part of her nature
that longed for isolation occasionally, to be quiet and
alone with her thoughts. And perhaps it was this
need, coupled with all the worries and problems of
her teens, that had given Purdey the air of indepen-
dence and self-confidence that had helped to get her
this job. But the worries were largely over now, thank
goodness; Toby's operation had been a success,
although he would always need strong glasses. He and
her mother were living in a pleasant flat in London,
and Mrs Bruce had a congenial office job that she
enjoyed. Purdey sent them money every month to
help out, but all that she could spare went into a
special account, which was still well short of its thirty-
five thousand pounds target, but was climbing all the
time. During the last two months the balance had
increased substantially because she hadn't had to pay
out any rent.

Purdey went through the gateway in the high wall
that separated the grounds of the dower house from
that of the hotel, and paused to look across at the sun
beginning to set in the evening sky. It would be a
great load off her mind and off her conscience when

that debt was at last paid. Maybe then she would be able to think of herself, perhaps take a proper holiday abroad somewhere instead of just going to stay with her mother and Toby. Although they would probably appreciate a holiday just as much as she would. She grew fanciful for a few moments, thinking where she would like to take them if she could afford it: Disney World for Toby of course, he longed to go; and Venice for her mother, and herself . . .? Purdey's imagination collapsed there; she had put holidays out of her mind for so long that she couldn't even dream about them any more.

The sun went behind a cloud, making her feel suddenly cold. With a shiver, Purdey pulled her coat round her and stepped out briskly now towards the hotel. The receptionist saw her coming and handed her her key. 'A few of the directors have already arrived,' he warned her. 'They're staying the night and will be eating in the main dining-room.'

Purdey thanked him and toyed with the idea of having dinner sent up to her room, but then decided to change and go down—you didn't get promotion by hiding from the directors! And if she met some of them socially this evening it might influence them a little in her favour when she read her report tomorrow. So she went up to her room, showered, and put on a long black velvet evening skirt and a cream silk shirt, brushed her hair up into a sophisticated pleat and added make-up and high heels. There, that should do it. Purdey inspected herself critically in the mirror and decided optimistically that she looked at least twenty-seven.

The head waiter, recognising her as a colleague,

gave her a friendly smile and led her to a table where Rob Willis, the hotel manager, was sitting to have his own meal. He stood as she came up and said, 'Hello, Purdey. I hope you don't mind sharing with me, but we're rather busy tonight.'

'Not at all. Is there something special on?'

'A captain's dinner for the local golf club.' He indicated a group of tables formed into a square in the partial privacy of one of the alcoves. 'And there are several of the directors dining in here tonight, so I want to be on hand to make sure everything goes smoothly.' He lifted a beckoning finger and a waiter was immediately at his side. 'What would you like to drink?'

'Perrier water, please.'

Rob grinned. 'Was that because I said the directors were here?'

'Not really. I don't drink much, anyway. But I admit I'd rather be completely sober if I should meet any of them. Although that isn't very likely, is it?'

'You never know. One of them is Simon Gascoyne; have you met him?' And, when Purdey shook her head, he went on, 'It was his family who originally owned this estate. It had been in the family for several centuries, evidently, but then two of the owners died soon after one another and they couldn't afford the death duties. So it was either sell it or give it to the National Trust. They decided to sell and were put in touch with a consortium of businessmen who were interested in establishing a chain of luxury hotels. They got their funding through a merchant bank and bought this place, but as part of the deal a member of the family was given a seat on the board.'

'An asset or a liability?' Purdey questioned.

'You get right to the heart of it, don't you?' Rob remarked appreciatively. 'As a matter of fact, he seems to be both. An upper-class playboy who's full of charm. He draws in a lot of customers by his contacts and because of the charm, but is quite likely to forget everything else and go off to a party in Mustique, or cruising in somebody's yacht for a month, whenever he gets invited.'

Purdey laughed. 'Well, I can't say that I entirely blame him. Life's too short not to make the most of it when you can.' There was a trace of wistfulness in her voice, but she covered it by saying quickly, 'How old is he?'

'Let's see, not much older than you, I should think. No, Simon Gascoyne can't be more than twenty-nine or thirty.'

They began their meal, and talked shop mostly, as Rob was interested in hearing about the other hotels she'd visited, but presently he interrupted her to say, 'Here are the directors now, six of them.'

But Purdey was sitting with her back to the room, and only caught the backs of a group of men in dinner-jackets as they were shown to their table. From that moment Rob's attention was fixed anxiously on the directors' table as he watched surreptitiously to make sure that everything was going well.

'Don't worry,' Purdey encouraged him. 'You know the hotel is superbly run.'

Rob shook his head. 'I still have nightmares about another hotel I was managing, where one of the staff suddenly went off his head and attacked the owner with a corkscrew.'

Purdey tried not to laugh, but couldn't resist it. Bob grinned and relaxed a little, but he still kept an eye on the other table. 'Are you in a hurry?' he asked her.

'No, I've got nowhere to go. Why?'

'Stay here with me, will you, until they've finished their meal? It gives me an excuse to stay in the dining-room.'

'Ah, so you had an ulterior motive in asking me to share the table. I ought to abandon you for that.'

'How about it if I bribed you with a second helping from the dessert trolley?'

'You obviously know the way to a working girl's heart. OK, I'll stay.'

So it was that they didn't leave their table until the group of directors had left theirs, following them out of the room only a couple of minutes later. Four of them had gone straight upstairs. Purdey caught a glimpse of what she thought must be them as they reached the top of the first flight and went through the door leading to the upper corridor. For a moment one of them seemed vaguely familiar, a tall, dark-haired man, but such a brief glimpse of his back view didn't recall anyone to mind and she let it go, thinking that she must either be mistaken or it was one of the men who had interviewed her for the job. The other two directors were standing in the inner foyer talking, and they looked up in recognition as Rob Willis, with Purdey by his side, walked towards them.

'An excellent meal,' the elder of the two congratulated him. 'Please give my compliments to the chef as usual.'

'And mine, of course,' the other man added. He was much the younger of the two, with rather long fair hair and a handsome, languid face. He was slim and young and very elegantly dressed, and Purdey had no trouble at all in identifying him as Simon Gascoyne. He looked Purdey over in open appreciation and said, 'Hello. I don't think we've met.'

Rob Willis obediently took his cue and said, 'This is Perdita Bruce, who recently joined the group as a marketing executive. Perdita, this is Charles Temple and Simon Gascoyne.'

They shook hands and Simon said, 'I heard they'd appointed their first female executive, but I had no idea you would be so attractive—and so young! At last I shan't feel so out on a limb.'

They all four talked together for a few minutes, but then the other director excused himself and Rob went off, at Simon's insistence, to tell the chef how much they'd enjoyed the meal. Purdey went to follow him but Simon caught her arm. 'Please don't go. My fellow directors have the advantage of me, you know. They know all about you and I don't. Come and have a drink and tell me all about yourself.' And he led her firmly into the lounge and over to a table in the bay window, part of the room but apart from it.

He ordered cognacs, overriding Purdey's protest, and gave her a charming smile. 'We can't possibly start our relationship on anything so mundane as Perrier water. It really ought to be champagne, but it's either too late in the evening or too early in the night for that. So we'll start with cognac and perhaps, who knows, we might progress to champagne later,' he said meaningfully.

Purdey gave him a quick glance, but was reassured by the amusement in his eyes. A flirt, but not to be taken seriously, she gathered. She smiled. 'Has that approach ever worked?'

'Ah, I'm afraid it would be very ungentlemanly of me to answer that question.' He grinned. 'Not to say immodest.'

'A lesson in how to answer a question without appearing to. Let me guess, I bet you're on the public relations side of the board.'

Simon burst out laughing. 'I can see I'm going to have to keep on the right side of you, or I shall have a formidable opponent.' Their drinks came and he raised his glass. 'To your success with the Tudor Rose Group, Perdita. May I call you that? It's a lovely name.'

'Thank you. And thank you for your good wishes, Simon.' She said his name naturally, not as if he was doing her any favour by coming down to the level of an employee. Because one day Purdey aimed to be a director of this company herself, and she intended to start by letting the directors know that she considered herself their equal. So if they called her by her first name she did the same, even if it startled those who were much older than she was. And besides, she intended to get on the board on her own merit, not by buying into it as Simon had done.

'You were going to tell me all about yourself,' he reminded her.

'No, that's what you said. You can find out all about me by reading my file. It's all there: qualifications and dates, experience and interests.'

'But that hardly tells me about the real you, does it? About the girl behind the facts. Why you chose a career instead of marriage and a family. And why you chose the hotel trade instead of modelling or acting or some other profession where looks like yours would have been a terrific asset.' He seemed genuinely interested, his eyes on her face as he spoke.

Purdey shook her head, ignoring the flattery. 'Why does anyone choose a certain career? You just take advantage of the opportunities that happen to come along when you're on the lookout. Most of life is pure chance, don't you think? If you hadn't happened to be in a certain place at a certain time, then your whole life might have been completely different.'

He nodded, an arrested expression in his eyes. 'Yes, I'm rather a fatalist myself.' His eyes ran slowly round the room, looking at the room itself as much as the people. 'If certain people hadn't died when they did, or if the tax laws were more humane, then my life would certainly have been different.'

He paused, and Purdey remembered that this had once been his family home. Did he resent having to come back here and see it being used in this way, with rooms he had thought of as his own being used by strangers? She said nothing, but he turned and caught her expression. 'You know about—the history of this place.' It was a statement, not a question.

'Yes, Rob Willis told me.'

His mouth twisted a little. 'I was destined for a course in estate management until my uncle and then my father died within two years of each other. There was nothing left then but to sell it or to give it to the nation in lieu of death duties. But the nation didn't want it and I ended up as a titular director.'

'But you work for the group, don't you?' Purdey asked in surprise.

'Oh, I try to earn my fees. Trouble is that old friends keep coming up with much more interesting ways to pass the time.'

'Tell me about them,' Purdey invited.

His eyebrows rose. 'You sure? Most of the people on the board go pale with horror at my exploits.'

'Are they that shocking?'

'Not shocking, no, just irresponsible. And everyone here is so upright and ambitious; they think taking off to go skiing or something for a few weeks is a major sin.'

'But I'm not one of the board,' Purdey pointed out. 'So tell me, how *do* the other half live?'

'Only when they can afford it, mostly.' But he started to tell her about his skiing trip and was soon talking happily, evidently much more at home in that other world than the one in which fate had plunged him. He was a good raconteur and Purdey was soon intrigued and enjoying herself, listening to stories of the sort of life she would never know. But she didn't feel envious at all, merely happy to enjoy it at second hand. Listening to him recalled Alex Nash to her mind and the time she'd worked at the gambling club. But that made her think of Jared Faulkner, and she pushed the thought away as she always tried to do, afraid to let her thoughts dwell on him.

She went on listening to Simon, but wasn't concentrating so completely now. After a while her thumbs began to prick and she felt uncomfortable, as if someone was watching her. Turning her head, she looked over her shoulder towards the bar and glimpsed a tall, dark man just leaving. He was the same man she'd seen earlier, and for a horrifying moment he reminded her of Jared. But no, it couldn't be. It was only that she had been thinking of him earlier that had brought the similarity into her mind.

She shuddered at the thought and Simon said, 'I'm sorry, I'm boring you.'

'No, not at all. Please go on. It was just that someone walked over my grave.'

Pushing the shadows of the past out of her mind, Purdey sat with Simon Gascoyne until almost midnight. She enjoyed being with him; he had a droll sense of humour that made her laugh, and his stories were just slightly over the top, which robbed them of any hint of snobbishness. And he was also experienced in handling women, setting out to intrigue and charm her, and so easy and relaxed in his manner that Purdey soon felt as if she'd known him for years instead of just hours. But, even though she was enjoying herself so much, at eleven-thirty she stood up resolutely and said, 'I'm afraid I must go. Thank you for the drink.'

'Must you really? The night's hardly begun.'

'Tomorrow is an important day for me—and I'd promised myself an early night.'

Simon got to his feet, his movements easy and graceful. 'Perhaps we can do it again some time, then? Have dinner or something.'

'Thank you, I should like that. Goodnight.' She held out her hand to shake his, but he took her hand and held it.

'Let me see you up to your room,' he said, smiling into her eyes.

But Purdey shook her head firmly. 'I'm quite sure I shall be perfectly safe.' But she returned the smile as she tried to withdraw her hand. 'Goodnight.'

But he carried it to his lips and lightly kissed her fingers before letting her go. 'Until tomorrow.'

She left him, feeling pleasantly tired and glad that she'd decided to come down to dinner. But she would have to be careful with Simon and not let him think that she was overkeen—she certainly didn't want the complication of having to fight off one of the directors! And, as charming and amusing as Simon was, Purdey already knew that he wasn't the right man for her. But then, she'd never been even friendly with one that was. Maybe one day, she thought, but then brushed the idea aside; she was a career girl, wasn't she? And career girls could manage without a permanent man to complicate their lives. No ties, no problems.

'Oh, Miss Bruce. There's a message for you.'

The receptionist's voice broke into her thoughts and she went over to the desk, expecting to be handed a note, but he said, 'There was a gentleman here earlier; he said he wanted to see you. He said he'd wait for you in the billiard-room.'

'When was this?' Purdey asked in surprise.

'Over an hour ago.'

'Did he give his name?'

'No.' The receptionist shook his head. 'He just said to be sure to give you the message.'

Purdey shrugged. 'Well, I hardly think he'll be there now, but I suppose I'd better go and look. I wonder why he didn't come and find me in the bar.' Mystified, wondering what could possibly be so urgent that anyone wanted to see her at this time of the night, Purdey walked quickly across the foyer and turned right, down the wide, carpeted corridor to the billiard-room. The light was on and there was the clicking sound of ivory billiard balls hitting together as she turned the handle and pushed open the door. But there was no match in play. A man stood alone, amusing himself by potting the balls as he waited. He had his back to her, and was tall and dark-haired. He turned, and Purdey stood frozen to the ground as Jared Faulkner said, 'Well, don't just stand there, Miss Bruce. Come in. I have something I want to say to you.'

Purdey's first instinct after that moment of stunned recognition was to turn and run. She took a half-step backwards, more in recoil than anything else, but Jared dropped the cue he was holding and strode quickly across to her, catching her wrist and pulling her into the room. Then he closed the door and leaned against it, a smile of mocking triumph twisting his lips. 'So we meet again,' he said menacingly.

Purdey stared at him, feeling sick inside. 'What—what do you want?' she managed.

'Why—to renew an old acquaintance, what else?'

His voice was silky, but she sensed an undercurrent of anger, scarcely suppressed. Trying to gather her whirling senses, she realised that she mustn't enrage him, but try to get away as quickly as possible. And she must be careful, she must let Jared think that she was only a guest here. If he found out that she worked for the hotel chain . . . Oh, lord, Purdey could just imagine it. 'Why—why here?' she asked, licking lips gone suddenly dry. 'You could have spoken to me in the bar.'

'You saw me there?'

She shook her head. 'No, not really. I caught sight of someone I thought looked familiar, but I wasn't sure. Now I realise it was you.'

'You really ought to be more on your guard, you know,' Jared said almost conversationally, but then his voice became suddenly savage as he added, 'Confidence tricksters like yourself ought to realise that the people they defrauded will be on the lookout for them. And wanting revenge.'

Purdey's head came up at that. 'I didn't *trick* you. You wanted something from me that you offered to pay for and you got it. That's all.'

He glared at her for a moment, then nodded. 'True. And I suppose I ought not to complain. But your price was a little too high for me to forget—or forgive.'

'But you paid it. You didn't have to.'

'And see a gold-digger like you married to Alex?' His lips twisted into a sneer. 'Hardly.'

'How is Alex?' Purdey asked with a catch in her voice.

Jared's eyebrows rose. 'Why? What does it matter to you?'

'He was a friend,' she said sharply. 'And I liked him a lot. Why shouldn't I ask how he is?'

'Because he's safely out of your clutches, and that's where he's going to stay. I suppose now you're going to tell me that I blighted the love of your life,' he remarked sardonically.

Her face tightening, Purdey looked at him antagonistically, her hatred showing despite all her opposite intentions. It had crossed her mind to tell him that she was saving up the money to pay him back, but she could imagine how he would laugh in sneering disbelief. No, when she sent the money back to him there would be just the cheque and nothing more. No letter of explanation, no excuses or reasons. Nothing. Just a grand gesture that would give him the slap in the face he deserved. Or so she'd always intended. But now she eyed him warily, wondering what *he* intended by this confrontation.

She didn't answer his gibe and he said, 'Just don't try to see Alex again, or it will be the worse for you.'

'I never have,' she repeated steadily. 'I kept my side of the bargain.'

A small frown flickered across his brows, but then his jaw hardened as Jared said, 'I should have thought thirty-five thousand was enough for you, but it seems you're still playing the same game.'

It was Purdey's turn to frown as she shook her head. 'I don't know what you mean.'

'Oh, don't try to act the innocent with me. I've seen the way you work. Remember? Seducing a young, rich man into falling for you, and then holding him at arm's length until he's so crazy for you that he proposes. So what do you intend this time? Is it marriage, or another pay off from his family?'

Her colour rising in anger, Purdey said forcefully, 'I don't know what you're talking about. Now, will you please get out of my way? I've had enough of this . . .'

But Jared reached out and caught her wrist, his eyes glaring into hers. 'I'm talking about Simon Gascoyne —as if you didn't know. Your latest dupe.' Purdey gasped, not only angry that he should be so mistaken, but shocked that he should know Simon. 'Yes, that startled you, didn't it? But I happen to know Simon rather well. It was my bank that helped finance the group that bought him out.'

Oh, hell! Purdey thought wretchedly. He was sure to tell Simon. But would Simon feel that he had to report it to the board? He might not, he might just like her enough not to. Or she could even tell him the truth, if she had the chance. But then she would be in Simon's debt. And she didn't want to be in anyone's debt. Not Simon's. Not Jared's. Oh, would she never be free? Fear giving her strength, Purdey managed to give a small shrug. 'You know him better than I do, then. I only met him tonight.'

'Is that true?' Jared demanded, eyes narrowing.

'Ask him yourself,' she said offhandedly, but praying that the two men wouldn't meet tomorrow. 'He spoke to me in the foyer after dinner and asked me to have a drink with him.'

'You didn't come here to be with him?'

'How could I, when I didn't know him?' She tried to pull her wrist away, but Jared continued to hold it in his steel-like grasp.

'Yes, but you're such an accomplished liar that I think it better not to believe you.'

'Suit yourself,' Purdey said angrily. 'And if you don't let go of me I'm going to start screaming. And you can talk your way out of that.'

'Threats?' His mouth twisted ironically. 'You seem to forget that I know the way to get to you.' And he put up his other hand to cup her chin and run his thumb across her mouth, his eyes cruel.

Purdey shrank back, her heart thumping painfully. So he remembered it too, that kiss, after all these years. But in such a different way. For him it was a means of subjugation, for her a devastation. A few seconds that had shaken her soul and influenced her life in the years between.

'So—now we both know you're not immune.' For a moment his grip tightened, but then he pushed her away from him as if she were dirty. 'How long are you staying here?' he demanded.

'Until—until tomorrow,' she lied.

Jared looked at her narrowly and then nodded. 'It had better be. But I shall check, so don't try any tricks. And I shall check to make sure you don't leave with Simon, so don't try that either.' He glared at her for a moment, then moved away from the door. 'All right, you can go.'

She glowered at him mutinously, wanting to tell him just what she thought of him, but wanting to get away even more. Stepping forward, she went to open the door, but as she reached it he put out an arm to bar her way. 'What was Simon going to be, then? A one-night stand?' Purdey flashed him a look of pure venom and he laughed harshly. 'You'll just have to go to bed hungry then, won't you?' And at last he let her go.

The good night's sleep that she'd wanted was now a hollow mockery. Purdey had to apply extra foundation colour to hide the dark shadows round her eyes when she got up the next morning. And she'd so wanted to be bright today, too. Damn Jared Faulkner! Purdey took hold of the edge of the washbasin and gripped it until her knuckles showed white. Why did he have to be here? Why? Just when everything was going so well, fate had to come and kick her to the ground again. But she had gone over that a hundred times already during the night, and it was no use dwelling on it. She just had to accept that fate had it in for her and learn to live with it.

Her churning stomach warned her to avoid breakfast, so she put on the suit she'd bought specially for today and went quickly down to reception, keeping an anxious eye out for Jared. But most of the guests were still having breakfast and she didn't see him. Going up to the desk, she beckoned over the female receptionist and said in a low voice, 'Please, could you do me a favour? There was a man last night who wouldn't leave me alone. I had to promise to meet him today to get rid of him. You know how it is. So if anyone asks for me, would you please tell him that I checked out and left the hotel very early?'

The receptionist looked sympathetic. 'No problem. It's happened before. What does he look like?'

'Tall and dark. Mid-thirties.'

'OK, leave it to me. I'll tell the others.'

'Thanks,' Purdey said gratefully, and hurried across the park to the safety of her own office. She made herself a coffee and tried to go over her report for one last time, but she couldn't concentrate. Her mind kept going back to Jared. Would he tell Simon? Her one hope was that he wouldn't because the story would show him up in a dubious light. And he would surely keep it secret in case Simon gossiped and it got back to Alex. That thought comforted her enormously, and it was with much happier spirits that she went along to wait outside the boardroom when ten o'clock came round and the meeting started. They didn't keep her waiting long. It was only ten-twenty when the managing director's secretary came out to get her.

The boardroom had once been the main dining-room of the house, and it still had the beautiful, long

Regency table that had been made for it. At least a dozen men sat round it now, but as Purdey followed the secretary she was only aware of a blur of faces turned towards her. She kept her eyes firmly on the managing director, whom she'd already met, as he rose to greet her. 'Good morning, Perdita. Here we are, I've saved you the seat next to mine,' he said amiably, and pulled the chair out for her.

But before they sat down, he said, 'We're all looking forward to hearing your report, but first I'd better introduce you to those of us you haven't met yet.' He introduced two men on the other side of the table and then Simon, who gave her a very friendly smile. Purdey was so relieved that she didn't look at the next man to be introduced until the chairman said, 'And I don't think you know our financial director, Jared Faulkner.' And Purdey found herself staring in stupefied disbelief into the malevolent eyes of the man who hated her!

CHAPTER THREE

PURDEY almost collapsed into her seat. She muttered
something and heard Jared's sardonic, 'We've already
met,' in return, but it was all a blur. Thankfully the
chairman began to describe why he'd asked her to do
the study, and that gave her a few minutes in which to
desperately try to pull herself together. Strangely, for
the moment she didn't feel angry or even resentful.
He was here, he was a director on the board, and that
was that. She was finished. Jared would have a quiet
word with the chairman and she would be asked to
leave. The first woman executive they'd ever had and
dismissed within three months, and now they'd
probably never employ another woman at that level
again. The old boy network and chauvinism at their
worst.

It was feminism that came to her rescue now. As
Purdey sat there, her hands gripped together in her
lap, she was filled with a flame of indignation and
determined to go down fighting. If she was going to
be fired, then she was going to go in a blaze of glory.
Not stammering over her report in fear and dread, but
giving it everything she'd got and making it the best
thing she'd ever done. So when the chairman came to
the end of his preamble a few moments later and
turned to her, saying, 'So let's hear what Perdita has
to say,' she rose to her feet in outward calm, only the

slight flush of colour on her pale cheeks betraying her inner torment.

She spoke clearly and concisely, illustrating her report with duplicated fact sheets which she passed round the table. Afterwards there were questions, many of them, but none that she hadn't anticipated, not even the ones that Jared threw at her. And then it was all over and the chairman was congratulating her, and Simon led the round of spontaneous applause that followed. She smiled, thanked them, and walked out able to hold her head high. She'd done it. She'd had her moment of glory, even if there was only humiliation to come.

But when Purdey reached her office the adrenalin suddenly ran out. She dropped her files of papers on the desk and fell into her chair, her head in her hands.

'Are you all right?' Sue asked, following her in. 'Didn't they like your report?'

'What? Oh, yes—yes, I think they did. It's just reaction now that it's all over, I suppose. I—Sue, would you mind, could you get me a strong black coffee?'

'Of course. Be back in a minute.'

The coffee tasted good, reminding her that she hadn't eaten yet, but she had no appetite for food. Sue tactfully left her alone, and as soon as some strength came back into her limbs Purdey got up and went to the window. She loved this view so much, looking out over the gardens and the park. Before her father had died they had had a small terraced house with a pocket handkerchief garden, but she had loved even that, spending her pocket money on packets of seeds and plants. That was what had so attracted her to this job, the chance of having an office here in these beautiful surroundings. Turning, Purdey looked at her desk and wondered if she ought to start clearing it. But she had been here such a short time that there were very few of her personal belongings in the room, just a photo of her mother and Toby, and a miniature rosebush that Toby had given her for her last birthday, both of which went everywhere with her. All her other possessions, apart from clothes, were packed up in boxes and stored at her mother's flat until she could get a place of her own.

A place of her own! Thanks to Jared that was again becoming an impossible dream. Now she would have to go through the process of finding another job from the extremely disadvantageous position of having been dismissed from this one after such a short time. A cold shiver ran through her as it occurred to Purdey that Jared might even be vindictive enough to stop her getting a similar post. He was a partner in a merchant bank and the director on several boards; with all his contacts he was probably quite capable of spreading the word not to employ her. So where did that leave her? To take a menial job well below her capabilities, or perhaps to emigrate. But she couldn't do the latter, no way could she leave her mother and Toby to manage without her.

Purdey finished her coffee and after a while went to get herself another. There was work that she could do, but what was the point? Glancing at her watch, Purdey tried to work out how long it would be before Jared came to tell her she was fired. That it would be Jared and not the personnel manager she was quite certain; anyone as pitiless as he wouldn't miss an opportunity like that to gloat over her. She was tempted to go now, to just go back to the hotel, pack up her things and disappear, but Purdey hadn't ever run away from her responsibilities yet, and she wasn't about to let someone like Jared Faulkner push her into it.

So, the board meeting would go on until at least twelve-thirty, which was soon, and then would break for lunch which would be served to them in the same room: snow-white linen, silver and crystal glass on that elegantly graceful table. That would be the first opportunity for Jared to tell the chairman about her—unless he'd already announced it to the full board. Maybe he wouldn't get the opportunity until after lunch, and enjoy prolonging her agony. But today, some time, he would come.

Purdey waited tensely till one o'clock, then in a burst of rebellion put on her jacket and went out for a walk in the park, careful to keep out of sight of the boardroom windows. She stayed out in the spring sunshine for a long time, and it was perhaps the hardest thing she ever had to do when she at last reluctantly turned and went slowly back to her office.

It had been breezy outside and golden tendrils had escaped from Purdey's drawn-back hair, but she didn't bother to comb them into place. She got herself yet another coffee, holding the beaker between her hands and forgetting to drink it as she stood at the window—waiting.

It was almost four o'clock before he came. They must have resumed the board meeting after lunch—to discuss her dismissal?—but now it was over and she saw the directors' cars passing as they left. Behind her she heard the door open, but didn't turn round.

Jared came in and shut the door, stood for a moment, his hands in his pockets, watching her. Then he said, 'It seems I underestimated you.'

Slowly Purdey turned to face him. 'I suppose you're going to elaborate on that.' Her voice was quite composed and unemotional. It could have been any conversation, except for the pallor in her face.

'I've been reading your file,' he said bluntly. 'I had no idea you're so talented. In fact, I could hardly believe I was reading about the same person. A college graduate—and a distinguished degree at that.'

'It's easy enough to check up on,' Purdey said sharply.

'It already has been checked.' Again that flickering frown. 'I take it you were going to college while you were working at the gaming club?'

Purdey looked at him defiantly for a moment, then nodded briefly. 'Yes.'

'So you were working your way through college. Very laudable.' She gave him a swift look, hearing the sarcasm behind the compliment. And she was right, because Jared went on forcefully, 'But that doesn't give you the right to extort money from others to pay for your education.'

Anger swept through her and Purdey strode towards him. 'I did not extort money from you! You came to me. You *offered* me money.'

'But that's exactly what you intended to happen. At first I thought you were a common tart who'd latched on to Alex by accident, but now I realise that you were a whole lot cleverer than that. You must have gone into his background and realised that he was the heir to a fortune, and that his family would have done anything rather than let him marry you. Either way you stood to gain. That's why you set your price so high—not because you were offended by the offer, even though you pretended you were, but because you knew just how much you could get away with.' Jared paused, his eyes glinting with anger. 'I bet you had no intention of marrying Alex, did you?'

Purdey glared at him for a moment, but then let her eyes fall, unable to hide the truth.

'So,' Jared said on a fierce note of suppressed rage, 'I was taken for an even bigger con than I thought.'

'For an even bigger fool!' Purdey shot at him, wanting to hurt and having nothing to lose.

His rage erupted suddenly and Jared grabbed her, catching hold of her arm and pulling her roughly against him. 'You little bitch! You've lied and schemed once too often. I'm going to teach you a lesson you won't ever forget.'

He tried to twist her round and bend her over his knee, but Purdey struggled wildly, terrified of being held close to him like this. 'No! Let me go. *Please!* Please let me go.'

Something of the terror in her voice must have got to him, because Jared became suddenly still, his breathing ragged. He still had hold of her but she held herself rigidly stiff, and after a moment he let her go and stepped back. 'Hell,' he said thickly, 'why is it that you . . .' He broke off and ran a hand through his hair. 'I apologise,' he said shortly. 'It's always a mistake to descend to violence, even if provoked into it by a common little slut like you.' He paused, then said gratingly, 'But you're not so common after all, are you? And perhaps not even a slut. Just a very clever con artist.'

Slowly Purdey turned to face him, and said dully, 'Why don't you just say what you came to say and then go?'

'And what do you think that is?'

She gave a harsh laugh. 'It's perfectly obvious. You have me in your power. In the hollow of your hand, where you can so easily crush me.' And she held out her cupped hand and pressed the other down on to it in demonstration. 'You had no hesitation in getting me fired from my job at the gaming club, so I'm quite sure you're deriving great satisfaction in getting me fired from this one. But then, sadistic pleasure is your forte, isn't it?'

'Yes,' he said, 'I do have you in my power. But just letting you walk away now is too easy. Now that I've found you, I think it will be better to keep an eye on you. I still don't trust you where Simon Gascoyne is concerned. You've already made quite an impression on him from the way he was singing your praises this morning. And after the brilliant way you gave that report at the board meeting, you're in the directors' good books too. If it hadn't been for that . . . But I'm sure I don't have to tell you. It's exactly the way you planned, isn't it? And I must admit I have to admire you,' he added unexpectedly. 'Only someone with exceptional nerve could have carried that off the way you did in those circumstances.'

Purdey stared at him, unable to believe that he was giving her a reprieve. But she might have guessed that it would be barbed with thorns. His mouth twisting sardonically, Jared went on, 'But don't think that

I've given up. I'm still going to make you pay for what you did, even if I do have to wait a while. You only have to step out of line once, and I'll tell my colleagues all about you.'

'Even if it means Alex finding out?'

'Are you threatening to tell him?'

Purdey's chin came up, her mind filled with hope. 'I might. If you don't keep your side of the bargain, why should I keep mine?'

He laughed harshly. 'You were no bargain—you were damned expensive! But go ahead and tell Alex, if that's what you want. He's more than over you, and it might do him good to learn the type of woman he fell for. Although I very much doubt if he'll even listen to you now after the way you walked out on him.'

She gave him a swift glance. 'What did you tell him?'

'Wouldn't you like to know?' Jared taunted. 'If you ever meet Alex again, you'll have to ask him. But I don't advise you to try it, because that would definitely be stepping out of line.'

'So I'm to go on here, but only under your sufferance?'

'That's right.'

'It would be better to leave right now,' she burst out.

'Then do so, by all means,' Jared answered in mocking cordiality. 'I'm sure the managing director will enjoy hearing your reasons for resigning.'

She stared at him, realising that he was playing with her, a game of cat and mouse in a circle of mousetraps. Whichever way she moved, he would be there, watching, tormenting, until he grew tired of the game and pushed her into a trap. 'You sadistic swine!' she said bitterly.

His eyes grew cold. 'Just watch your manners, you little tramp. I don't take that from you.'

'No, but I have to take your insults, don't I? Well, if you call me names, then I'm going to do the same. And at least my insults have the merit of being the truth.'

'Oh, really?' He strode forward and put his hand on her neck. 'Just try it, that's all.'

Purdey wrenched herself away from him, her heart beating wildly. 'You do all this to me and you haven't even bothered to ask *why*!' Gathering what little dignity she had left, she faced him and said, 'You've done what you came to do, now get out of my office. *Go on, get out.*'

Jared looked at her balefully but, recognising the note of hysteria in her voice, he turned on his heel and went to leave, then checked and picked up the photo of her mother and Toby from the desk. 'Who are they?'

Quickly she snatched it from him and held it close to her chest, her arms across it protectively. 'Mind your own damn business.'

His jaw thrusting forward, Jared said gratingly, 'You'll say that once too often.' Then his eyes went deliberately to the photograph frame. 'But it seems I've found *another* weakness of yours.' And on those words, uttered in such a threatening tone, he left her alone at last.

Purdey gave him ten minutes to get clear of the building, then grabbed up her jacket, said a hurried goodbye to her startled secretary and hurried back to the hotel. She wanted to go straight up to her room, but the receptionist on duty called her over to give her a small bundle of notes and letters. Purdey took them and turned to go, but almost bumped into Rob Willis, the manager.

'Hello, Purdey. Well, how did it go?' he asked when she didn't speak.

'Oh, OK, I think. Rob, if you'll excuse me . . .'

'Are you all right? You don't look very well.'

'No. I've—I've got rather a bad headache.' Which was quite true; from the moment when Jared had left her, Purdey's head had felt as if she had a knife piercing into her brain.

'Need some medical help?'

'No. I'll be fine.'

'How about a brandy, then?'

'No!' Her voice rose sharply and she bit her lip. 'Oh, Rob, I'm sorry. I just want to go up to my room and lie down.'

'Of course. I'm the one who should apologise. Here, I'll walk you up there.' Taking her arm firmly, in case she decided to faint, Rob walked with her to the lift and then along the corridor to her room. 'Got your key?' She gave it to him and he opened the door and escorted her inside. 'Well, here's something to cheer you up,' he remarked.

Following his glance, Purdey gave a little gasp of surprise and pleasure as she saw an exquisitely arranged bowl of flowers standing on a low table in the centre of the room. 'Oh, how lovely!' Going forward, she gently touched the petals of a pale yellow iris and bent to smell the scent of some early roses.

'You obviously have an admirer,' Rob told her.

'Aren't you going to open the card?' And he indicated a small envelope propped against the base of the arrangement.

'In a moment; I think I know who they're from.'

'I'll leave you, then. But remember, ring the desk if your head gets worse or you feel ill.' He hesitated, obviously undecided, then said curiously, 'Purdey, why are you clutching that photograph frame?'

She gave him a startled glance, then realised that she still had the photo clutched tightly in her left hand, against her breast. With a self-conscious laugh, she said, 'Oh, I—I decided to keep it here instead of the office.'

Rob smiled. 'I hope it's of the chap who sent you the flowers.'

He left her and she slowly put the photo on the table beside her bed. It would be safer there. Jared wouldn't be able to come here and search out her weaknesses. Purdey looked at the photo and smiled a little—or her strengths. She gave the glass a polish with her finger, then picked up the card. It was from Simon, as she'd supposed. 'Thank you for a most pleasant evening. Congratulations on this morning. Will call you for that dinner date. S.'

A note that would have gratified her had it been a day earlier, but Jared had warned her to keep away from Simon, so she would have to refuse to go out with him when he phoned her. Damn Jared! How dared he dictate to her like this?

Going into the bathroom, Purdey took some aspirins to try to ease her headache, than pulled the curtains and lay down on the bed. But, despite her sleepless night, she found it impossible to even doze.

She tried to think the problem through logically, as she'd been taught at college, without letting emotion enter into it. But whenever she thought of Jared her pulses throbbed with anger and a deep-down, scarcely recognised emotion that was half fear, half a fascinated awareness. She was still amazed that she hadn't been sacked on the spot, but remembered the impression her report had made on the board and began to think that for the moment she might possibly have the upper hand. In other words, she was proving too useful an employee for Jared to dare to suggest getting rid of her. Which was fine as long as she could keep up the standard of her work. But, as she'd always intended to do that anyway, it was really no problem.

Which left only Jared's threats about stepping out of line. Just what did 'stepping out of line' entail? she wondered. Going out with Simon, obviously. Well, OK, she could give up that in order to keep her job. And seeing Simon might have led to complications anyway, although she had no doubt of her ability to handle him. So what did that leave? All she could think of was contacting Alex again, which she had no intention of doing. Apart from that, Purdey could think of nothing that Jared could hold over her, which made her feel more cheerful. And, although Jared could check on her work easily enough, he couldn't possibly spend enough time here at the group's head office to watch her private life very closely. No, although his threats had been uttered with such force, they were largely empty ones. and the longer he had to hold back any disclosures about her, the better it would be, Purdey realised. She would gain the time to establish herself as a valuable member of the staff, and the longer she kept the job the better it would look on her employment record.

Her headache eased as Purdey began to relax and her mind drifted a little. She remembered Jared's fierce anger when she'd called him a fool, and her own fear when he had caught hold of her. But the fear hadn't been because he might hurt her, but in case he had the opposite reaction and took her in his arms to kiss her again. A fear not of him but of her own weakness. There had been other boyfriends since Alex, but none whose kisses could arouse her to such a flame of awareness as Jared's. No one that she wanted to go on holding and kissing and loving her, who could make her body come alive. No one else. And yet he was the one man in the world who had reason to hate and despise her. Heavens but life was ironic! Why did it have to be him, of all men? Or was that to be her punishment for taking his money? Was she to spend the rest of her life in frustrated yearning for something she had glimpsed once and was never to know again?

Purdey drifted into fitful sleep and dreamt of Jared filling all the glasses on the boardroom table with red poison and making the directors drink it. Only the poison was all lies about her, and when they'd drunk it they all turned on her and began to scream abuse and threaten her, while Jared stood in the background, smiling that cold, sardonic smile, his lips twisted in sadistic pleasure.

With a cry Purdey sat up in bed, her heart thumping wildly, her hair pricked up on her neck, and sweat on her face. Her hands were shaking as she raised them to her head, but then she quickly reached out to turn on the light and lift the enclosing darkness. A knock sounded at the door and she realised that it must have been what had awakened her. 'Just—just a minute.' Groping for her shoes, Purdey straightened her clothes and went to the door.

One of the waiters from the hotel dining-room stood outside with a food trolley. 'The manager found out you hadn't eaten today, Miss Bruce, so he's sent you up some dinner.'

'Oh, thanks.'

Purdey opened the door and he wheeled it in. 'And there are some telephone messages for you, too. Mr Willis thought they might be important.'

She thanked him again, but wished that she'd been left to go on sleeping. Until she caught the faint aroma of the hot food. Lifting the silver dish covers, Purdey found a quail's egg salad starter followed by grilled sole. Suddenly she felt hungry and sat down to eat, her spirits rising with each mouthful of the delicious food. There was a pudding and coffee too. Feeling much better, Purdey poured the coffee, and only then remembered the telephone messages. And there had been some letters for her earlier, too. Collecting them together, Purdey sat in an easy chair and began to go through them as she drank her coffee.

The first letter was from her mother, to say that she had been asked by the local Scoutmaster to take the place of his assistant, who had been taken ill and was unable to help with the weekend camping trip Toby was already booked to go on. Purdey had been planning to go home for the weekend, but there was little point if they were going away. She would stay here and perhaps explore the countryside a little, she

decided. The other envelope contained not letters, but
notes handed in at reception for her. There were three
of them, one from the personnel manager and another
from the managing director, both congratulating her
on her conference feasibility report. The managing
director even added that he was sure that she was
going to be a great asset to the group. Which pleased
Purdey immensely and made her understand even
more why Jared had had to hold his hand; if the
managing director had been that effusive to the other
directors, Jared would have looked pretty stupid
coming out with his story then.

The third envelope contained a note from Simon, or
rather an invitation. To go out with him on Saturday.
'I thought you might like to come and see me put in
some polo practice,' he suggested. 'And then we could
go out to dinner.' There was no mention of where the
polo practice was to take place or how she was to get
back to the hotel after dinner, Purdey noticed rather
wryly. Briefly she wondered if she had been a little too
forthcoming last night, had made it too obvious that
she enjoyed Simon's company. Sometimes men read
too much into it when you showed that you liked
them. But, in Purdey's book, liking someone didn't
equate with an immediate affair. She shrugged; it was
immaterial now anyway, because she wouldn't be
going out with him. The note gave a phone number
where Simon could be reached that evening, but
before ringing to refuse Purdey picked up the
telephone messages.

One of these was from her mother who, Purdey
guessed, wanted to know how she had got on today.
The other two were from Simon, the first just saying

that he had rung, and the second cancelling the number he'd given in his invitation and asking her to ring another number instead.

Purdey rang her mother first, and was careful to sound happy and cheerful, stressing how well everything had gone and reading out the notes of congratulation she'd had. Then they talked about the coming weekend, when Mrs Bruce was to help with the scout trip. 'Don't overdo it,' Purdey warned. 'Looking after a crowd of teenage boys will probably be exhausting. The Scoutmaster should have asked a man to go.'

Her mother laughed. 'I doubt if he could find one who was willing. But don't worry about me. Derek Wilson—he's the Scoutmaster—is quite capable of keeping them in order. He just can't watch them all at the same time.'

'Why didn't he ask his wife to help?'

'Oh, he isn't married.'

Her mother said it so casually that Purdey's ears immediately pricked up. 'What's he like?' she asked.

'Derek? Oh, he's a schoolmaster. At that public school where Toby goes for saxophone lessons. He's getting on really well at that, by the way. He can play "When the Saints Go Marching in" now.'

Purdey smiled and allowed herself to be sidetracked, but when she put the phone down she didn't know whether to be pleased or sorry. It was marvellous that her mother had met someone she liked, and it would be great if everything went well, but what if this Derek Wilson was a confirmed bachelor and her mother suffered yet another heartache? She sighed and decided that men just weren't worth it, and in that mood picked up the phone again to call Simon. She got through to his London club. The steward offered to have Simon brought to the phone, but Purdey said, no, she just wanted to leave a message. 'Will you tell him that Miss Bruce is unable to accept his invitation? Thank you.' And she put the phone down, glad that that danger at least was out of the way.

The next day was Friday, and Purdey had a morning meeting to discuss her ideas and findings with several middle-management people, the ones who put through the decisions made by the directors. All men, of course. The only other woman there was the secretary who took the minutes. They were impressed as the directors had been, but showed only surprise and not admiration. They had their own futures to think about, and didn't want any pushy female edging them out of the promotion hierarchy. And if she did they would immediately accuse her of using her sexuality, Purdey thought wryly. At the moment, though, they were friendly if wary, and as she wasn't treading on anyone's toes they were prepared to go along with her. The discussion lasted until lunchtime, and they decided to walk over to the hotel and continue over a snack there. Purdey slipped into her office first and found a memo from Sue: 'Mr Gascoyne rang and asked you to call him back.' Purdey frowned, hoping that Simon wasn't one of those men who wouldn't take no for an answer.

'If Simon Gascoyne rings again,' she told Sue on the way out, 'tell him I'll be unavailable for the rest of the day.' And she gave the same instuction to the operator at the hotel. Which she hoped would make Simon realise that she wasn't going to change her mind.

That evening she went to see a film in the nearby town, determined to push Jared out of her mind as much as she possibly could. But he wasn't easy to shut out. She had the uneasy feeling that he wasn't going to just stand by and let her live her life unmolested now that he had found her again. Perhaps he would set someone to watch her, either at the office or at the hotel. Possibly both. She would have to be on her guard twenty-four hours a day, which wasn't a pleasant prospect at all. If only she could find a place of her own, at least she would be able to relax half the time. Determined to try, she bought a copy of the local paper the next morning and went to look at three places that were to let. But all three were in built-up areas, were very small and extremely over-priced. Dejectedly Purdey went back to the hotel set in those gorgeous grounds. It seemed that to find anywhere at a rent that would allow her to send some money to her mother and pay off Jared she would have to go back to sharing a house or even a room. She shrank from the thought but knew that it would have to be done, although it would be doubly hard after her lovely room at the hotel. But at least she would still have the view from her office window and the grounds to walk in during the lunchbreak.

Purdey drew up in the hotel car park and walked into the entrance, her thoughts miles away. But then someone stepped in from of her and took hold of her arms. 'Hello, Perdita.'

She looked up, startled, but before she had time to speak Simon grinned, then bent to kiss her, right there in front of the whole hotel!

CHAPTER FOUR

'HEY!' Purdey pulled away from him angrily. 'Don't do that.'

But Simon was in no way perturbed. 'Mm, you look fabulous when you're angry.' And he gave her one of his boyish and most charming smiles.

'I suppose this is the point when most women melt at your charm,' Purdey said crossly, acutely aware of the grinning receptionists.

'But you're not going to?'

'Certainly not.' Turning, she walked down the corridor and went to go into the billiard-room, but remembered that was where she'd rowed with Jared and hastily went on to the next room, a small sitting-room that was used for cards in the evenings. It was empty now, all the guests at lunch or out for the day. Simon had followed her and she swung round on him. 'You shouldn't have done that.'

'But I enjoyed it very much.' He came to stand in front of her, looking quizzically down into her face. 'Why so angry, Perdita? It was no big thing.'

She bit her lip, realising that from his point of view it was true. But there was no way she could explain. 'No, I know. I'm sorry. It's just that—that I'm an employee here.'

'Ah, I begin to understand.' Simon took her by the elbow and led her over to two armchairs set in the

74

bow window. 'But you didn't object to sitting in the bar and having a drink with me a few nights ago,' he reminded her.

'Yes, but—well, that was before . . . That was different.'

'How—different?'

'Oh, forget it. Let's leave it. Just—just don't do it again, OK?'

Tilting his head slightly to study her face, Simon said, 'Sorry, but when you look as lovely as you do today, with your hair loose like that, it's a promise I might not be able to keep.'

He was trying to charm her, Purdey knew, but she said shortly, 'In that case, it would obviously be better if we didn't see each other again.'

'Ouch! Hoist with my own petard, to use a hackneyed phrase. Perdita,' Simon leant forward and took her hand, 'won't you tell me what's the matter?'

'There's nothing.'

'But I think there is. Why won't you come out with me?'

She shook her head agitatedly. 'I—can't.'

'Can't? Not won't? Well, that's something at least.' He looked at her searchingly. 'You're not already married to a twenty-stone all-in wrestler, are you?' he asked in mock alarm.

Purdey gave an involuntary smile. 'No, of course not.'

'That's better.' Simon gave her one of his devastating smiles. 'So, please, won't you tell me what *is* the matter?'

He would have to have some explanation, Purdey realised, so she compromised with a half-truth. 'I've been warned off you.'

His eyebrows shot up in surprise. 'Good heavens, is my reputation that bad?'

Purdey laughed. 'Well, you should know. Is it?'

'Certainly not, it's all lies made up by jealous rivals.' He gave her a keen look and she suddenly realised that there was an alert mind behind the nonchalant exterior. 'So why were you warned off and who did the warning?'

'We were seen together on Wednesday night,' she explained reluctantly. 'And it was pointed out to me that—that it wasn't company policy for employees to—er—mix socially with the management.'

'What utter rubbish!' Simon exclaimed. 'I've heard nothing of it. Who saw us?'

Purdey shook her head. 'I'm not going to tell you.'

'Aren't you, indeed? Well, whoever it was, he's an out-of-date old fool,' Simon said feelingly. 'And I shall make my feelings known at the next board meeting.'

'No, please, I'd much rather you didn't.'

'But, Perdita, I . . .'

'Purdey,' she interrupted. 'My friends call me Purdey.'

Simon smiled. 'Thank you. Why don't you want me to say anything?'

'It's very simple; I want to keep my job.' He started to protest, but she held up a hand. 'Please try to see it from my point of view. I'm the first woman the Group has recruited at junior management level. I'm very new and very much on probation. How do you think the other directors will feel if they think I'm—socially involved with you? I like you, Simon, but I want to keep this job, so if they don't want me to go out with you then I have to go along with that. I'm sorry.'

He frowned. 'Yes, I understand. But I still think it's a downright Victorian policy.' Thrusting his hands into his pockets, Simon walked over to the window and looked out moodily, evidently trying to think of some way round her imaginary ban. 'I was hoping we could have lunch together. You haven't eaten yet, have you?'

'No, I came back to the hotel to have something.'

An idea occurred to him and Simon said eagerly, 'Why don't we go somewhere else for lunch?' He held up a hand as Purdey opened her mouth to protest. 'We'll go in separate cars, of course, and meet up at the restaurant. What do you say, Purdey? Why should we let a parcel of narrow-minded old fogies force us apart? After all, we only want to enjoy each other's company over a meal.'

His description hardly fitted Jared, but then Simon wasn't to know that. Purdey was greatly tempted, her anger at the embargo on her freedom far greater than Simon's annoyance, but she shook her head regretfully. 'I can't risk it, Simon. What if someone saw us?'

'Who's to see? None of the directors live round here. But I tell you what . . .' He snapped his fingers as inspiration came to him. 'I know a place where I can guarantee that no one will see us.'

'Where? Don't forget that there are people who work in the office who do live round here and might be at a local restaurant.'

He shook his head, highly pleased with himself. 'Not a restaurant. We'll go to my cousin's place. He and

his wife have a house only about eight miles away.
We'll go there for lunch.'

'But we can't just turn up without any warning,'
Purdey protested.

'Of course we can. They'd love to have us.'

Purdey had to smile at his confidence. Belatedly she
remembered that she didn't want to get involved with
Simon, but that was something you tended to forget
when you were with him. He was so open and
charming, you just couldn't help liking him. Deciding
to be frank, Purdey said, 'Look, Simon, I enjoy your
company, but I have to tell you straight out that—
well, that I'm not in the market for anything more
than friendship.'

'Concentrating on your career?' he asked with
raised eyebrows.

'Something like that.'

Moving to stand beside her, Simon looked down
into her face. 'You're not a man-hater, are you?' But
then he answered his own question. 'No, you can't be,
not with a face and figure like yours. You're made to
be loved, Purdey. Is there a man in your life?'

She gave a small negative shake of her head. 'No.'

'And yet you want nothing more than friendship.
Why is that? I wonder. What a mystery woman you're
becoming.' He lifted his hand to stroke her cheek, but
Purdey backed off and he gave a reluctant sigh. 'OK.
If that's what you want. I'm willing to settle for
friendship—for now.' He gave a boyish grin. 'But I
reserve the right to try and persuade you to change
your mind. Now,' he went on before she could
protest, 'I'm going to drive away from here while you
go up to your room for five minutes, then you follow

me. Turn right when you reach the main road, and you'll find me waiting in a lay-by about a mile further on. Then we can go in convoy to my cousin's house.'

Purdey hesitated again, but then nodded. The morning had been so depressing that she needed some company, and it would be nice to visit a proper home after living in hotels for the last few weeks. And it would be safe enough at Simon's cousin's; there would be no prying eyes to be afraid of there, no one to report back to Jared. 'All right, we'll do it.'

'Great. See you in ten minutes.'

Purdey took rather longer than that because she took the opportunity to change and touch up her make-up, but she was soon following Simon's white Jaguar down the driveway to a sprawling old farmhouse framed by trees, the different levels of its windows and gables telling the story of its growth over the centuries. They parked the cars on the gravel sweep that circled a gnarled walnut tree, and Simon took Purdey's hand to lead her up to the doorway at the right hand end of the house. His ring was greeted by the barks of dogs who rushed out to meet him as soon as the door was opened.

They were followed by Simon's cousin-in-law, Julia Gascoyne, and her two sons who all greeted Simon rapturously, showing no surprise at his turning up on the doorstep and demanding lunch.

'Come on in and pour us all a drink, Simon. Ned's around somewhere. I think he's trying to do something terrifically clever with the plumbing so that the shower in the bathroom works.'

She led the way into a huge farmhouse kitchen with a great scrubbed pine table in the centre and a big Aga cooker in what had once been an inglenook fireplace. The table was obviously meant for food preparation, but it was piled with newspapers, toys, cardboard boxes and a box of tools, until there was only a corner left where Julia was trying to prepare lunch. Purdey took one look and realised that the family must always live in a state of happy chaos, a state she found she envied with all her heart.

Simon brought them all drinks and then went off to look for his cousin.

'We're having Sunday lunch today,' Julia announced, 'because we're out tomorrow. The kids just love roast beef and Yorkshire pudding, but it takes such ages to prepare.'

She began to peel some potatoes, but had to stop to look at the beef and then open the door to let the dogs out, and help the youngest boy with a book he was trying to read. Purdey began to see why it took her so long, and firmly took the potato peeler out of her hand. 'Here, let me.'

'Oh, thanks. I'll do the Yorkshire puddings, although they never seem to rise.'

Within ten minutes Purdey had taken over the meal and the two girls were chatting like old friends. Julia was like Simon, completely casual and easy to get along with because they accepted people for what they were. Julia asked no status-establishing questions of her; she was just Simon's girlfriend and welcome as such. Her husband, Ned, came into the kitchen about half an hour later dressed in greasy jeans and a sweater. He was obviously shrewder than Julia, but greeted Purdey just as amiably. He was evidently used to the havoc in the kitchen and as clearly in love with his wife, for he came to put his arm round her as they all had another drink.

It turned out to be the latest lunch Purdey had ever eaten, but definitely one of the most relaxed and enjoyable. There was a lot of laughter and a couple of heated discussions in which Purdey more than held her own, putting her view with succinct clarity, but without trying to browbeat anyone. Not that she would have had much chance in that company, where everyone was used to airing their own opinions. The Gascoynes had accepted her before, but after the meal Purdey had the feeling that they genuinely liked her. Because she hadn't been afraid to speak her mind? Or perhaps because they were surprised she had a mind at all, if a remark Julia made when they were clearing up after the meal was anything to go by. As Purdey brought a tray of glasses into the kitchen, Julia said, 'Oh, thanks. It's good of you to help. Some of the girls Simon brings over are terrified of spoiling their clothes or breaking their nails. And they nearly always just sit and smile and look beautiful. Perhaps he's growing up at last.'

Purdey laughed. 'Ah, but I'm not actually a girl-friend, you see. I'm really only a colleague.' And she told Julia about her job at the hotel.

'And you actually live at the hotel?' the older girl asked.

'Until I can find a place of my own. Although I'll still have to do a lot of travelling even then.'

'Have you looked at much yet?'

'As a matter of fact I looked at some this morning, but they weren't suitable,' Purdey answered, making light of it.

When they'd finished clearing up, they all went for a walk in the gardens. Once this had been the heart of a very large farm, but succeeding owners had gradually sold off parcels of land until now there were only a few acres, mostly of paddocks and overgrown garden. Purdey gathered that the Gascoynes had only bought the place a couple of years ago, and they still had a London flat where they spent most of their time. Ned worked in the city and the boys went to primary school there, so the farm was really their weekend and holiday place, and so got rather neglected.

They split up as they walked round, Purdey walking first with Simon as Julia talked to her husband, and then with Ned and the boys after Julia called Simon over.

'Come and look at our cottage,' Julia invited as she and Simon joined them again. 'It used to be the Tudor wash-house, but it was converted into a staff cottage in the 1920s.'

It was a pretty little place with flint-stone walls and latticed windows, and a door so low that Simon bumped his head and swore. Inside there was a small bedroom, a sitting-room, kitchen and tiny bathroom, but it was nicely decorated, and furnished with modern but comfortable pieces.

'We've been trying to get a housekeeper,' Julia remarked. 'But we've had no luck so far.' She turned to Purdey. 'Actually, we wondered if you'd be interested.'

'But—but I already have a job,' she explained in surprise.

'Yes, but you said you wanted somewhere to live

and we thought perhaps you could keep an eye on the place for us and do some occasional baby-sitting instead of paying rent. Unless you think you'd be afraid to live here alone, of course.'

'Why, no. I—it's very kind of you. I'm afraid you've taken me completely by surprise.'

'Why don't the two of you sit down and discuss it?' Ned suggested. 'Come on, Simon, let's leave them to it.'

But Purdey didn't need much convincing or persuading; the cottage, which was about thirty yards from the house, would be ideal for her. The setting was lovely and it was in easy driving distance from the office. But the clincher of course was that she could act as caretaker instead of paying any rent, which meant that she could pay off the money she owed Jared that much quicker. 'But you do realise that I have to do quite a lot of travelling in my job?' she warned.

'Yes, but the summer holidays are coming up so we'll be here more often. I'm happy to give it a try if you are,' Julia said firmly. 'And you'd really be doing us a big favour.'

'All right. Thanks. When would you like me to move in? I can come as soon as you like.'

'Come tomorrow, then,' Julia answered promptly. 'There's no point in waiting.'

So, as she drove back to the hotel later that evening. Purdey found that her life had taken a sudden change for the better. She liked the Gascoynes, all four of them, very much, and knew that she was going to love living in the cottage. The one drawback, of course, was that she would be accessible to Simon, but she had made it plain that she didn't want to get involved with him, and he would have to learn to accept that. She glanced in her rear-view mirror and saw his white sports car behind her. Simon had insisted on seeing her safely back to the hotel before he drove to London. The hotel entrance came into sight and she turned into the driveway and parked in a small car park at the side of the hotel reserved for staff.

Purdey got out and wasn't at all surprised to see that Simon had followed her. Taking her hand, he drew her down a path in the garden to a small summerhouse by the lake, walking forward surely in the darkness.

'I've an idea you've been here at night before,' Purdey remarked.

'Of course. I used to live here. This was a favourite place for illicit midnight feasts and swimming parties when I was a boy.'

'And now that you're a man?'

'It's a very good place for saying goodnight to a girl properly.' And he bent to kiss her.

It was a very nice kiss. Simon was very experienced and knew exactly how to arouse a girl. Only he didn't arouse her. To Purdey it was just a kiss. His lips didn't send any flame of desire running through her veins. They didn't create any aching need to hold and be held. There was no feeling of drowning, or the fierce urgency of passion. Purdey did her best to respond, hoping that a miracle might happen again, but it was just a passing pleasure and nothing more.

For her anyway, but for Simon it was obviously better, because he wanted to go on kissing her and she had to firmly push him away. 'Hey, I said just friends.

Have you forgotten already?'

'Mm? You know you didn't mean it.'

'Oh, but I did. Behave yourself, Simon. You're as bad as Alex was.'

'Alex?' Simon lifted his head to look at her. 'Who's Alex?'

'Someone I used to go out with years ago who wouldn't take no for an answer, either.'

'Really? He sounds like a sensible chap. What was his name?' And he bent to kiss her throat.

'Alex Nash. Simon, stop it, or I'll go in. I . . . What is it?' she asked as she saw his look of surprise.

'I know Alex Nash. We were at school together. He's a couple of years or so younger than me, but his mother and mine are friends, so I used to see quite a lot of him. Did you know him well?'

'Not really,' Purdey answered hollowly, wishing she'd kept her mouth shut. 'We only went out together for a few months. It was while I was at college.'

'But he wouldn't take no for an answer, wouldn't he?' Simon grinned. 'The young devil.'

'It wasn't what you think,' Purdey said quickly. 'We were friends, that's all.'

'Oh, quite.' But Simon didn't look as if he believed her. 'I think he's back in England now. He's been travelling around learning various aspects of farming and estate management for the last few years.'

He looked as if he was going to ask her more questions, so Purdey quickly looked at her watch. 'I'd better go in. I shall be busy tomorrow, moving into the cottage.'

'Sure you don't want any help with that?'

'No, thanks,' Purdey said firmly. 'I can manage.'

He insisted on kissing her again, but eventually let her go and they parted in the car park, Purdey going up to her room in a far happier frame of mind than she'd felt that morning.

During the following two weeks her luck seemed to hold; Purdey moved into the cottage and soon established a routine of going round the Gascoynes' farmhouse twice a day to make sure that everything was OK. They had a cleaner who came in every Monday, but Purdey watered the half-dead pots of plants, threw out unused food from the fridge, and did lots of little things that made a world of difference to the old house. It needed a family there all the time, she thought. It was much too beautiful to be so neglected. At work, things went well too; there were lots of meetings with the heads of various departments, and eventually it was decided to go ahead with providing conference facilities as a prototype venture at the company's hotel at St Helier in Jersey, the largest of a group of islands in the English Channel near the coast of France.

An architect was sent over to draw up outline plans for the extension that would have to be built, and a copy of them soon arrived on Purdey's desk. She took them back to the cottage to study one evening, turning off a sports programme on television to do so, but the programme must have lingered in her mind, because as she looked at the plans it occurred to her that sport and leisure centres were now a growing industry. Why not incorporate one into the hotel complex to offer a complete service for conference guests, not just food and accommodation, but leisure facilities for them and their families too? That way the business conference could combine with a family holiday. As Purdey turned the idea over in her mind, she became more excited by it. But she couldn't just come up with the idea, she must have reasons to back it. Picking up a notepad, Purdey quickly began to jot down ideas and questions she must ask the Jersey tourism bureau when she phoned them first thing tomorrow morning.

It took some very long telephone calls to Jersey and some very fast and concentrated work, but by the early afternoon of the next day Purdey was ready to put her ideas to the management. First of all she showed it to her immediate boss, who was gratifyingly keen on the idea. 'It will probably be a matter of finance,' he warned her. 'Leave it with me and I'll put it to the directors. There should be a couple in today.'

So Purdey rather reluctantly handed over her brainchild, and didn't expect to hear any more about it for a few days, but was surprised when her boss put his head into her office a couple of hours later and told her that he'd shown her project to a member of the board who wanted to discuss it with her.

'Really?' Purdey got quickly to her feet. 'What did he say? Was he interested?'

'Presumably. Come on, he's waiting.'

They began to walk quickly down the corridor into a wing given over entirely to the directors' offices, and went up the stairs to the first floor. 'Who did you show it to?' Purdey asked. 'The promotions manager?'

'No, he isn't in. As it would cost such a lot of money, I decided to show it to the finance director first.' And he stopped outside a door with the name 'Jared Faulkner' on it, gave a firm knock and opened the door for her to go in.

Purdey stood stock-still and stared at him, but it was too late now to back out. Glancing past him, she saw Jared sitting behind a large antique desk, a mocking smile twisting his lips. 'Do come in, Miss Bruce,' he invited.

Slowly Purdey walked forward, feeling like a fly walking towards a praying mantis. He nodded to her boss, who left them alone. Jared didn't get to his feet, merely sat back in his chair and looked at her, his hands steepled together. She returned his gaze, realising that her leisure centre idea was doomed from the start, she might just as well tear it up now and throw it in the wastepaper basket. Jared gestured towards a chair but she remained standing, her chin lifting with a defiant tilt.

His lips curled a little, but he pointed to her carefully worked-out paper. 'So you've come up with another bright idea.' There was nothing for Purdey to say to that, but she knew that he would have some comment. She didn't have long to wait. 'Trying to ingratiate yourself further with the company?' Jared said derisively.

Stepping forward, Purdey reached out to snatch up her report from his desk, her eyes aflame with anger, but Jared's hand shot out and he caught her wrist. 'Put it down,' he commanded.

'Why? So that you can have the pleasure of destroying it? Don't worry; I already know that it's never going to go any further. At least, not as *my* idea.'

His eyes glinting dangerously, Jared's grip tightened

on her wrist, his fingers biting into her flesh. 'I said, put it down.' For a moment longer she defied him, but he increased the pressure until she gave a wince of pain and her fingers opened, the report falling back on his desk. 'Now, sit down,' he ordered shortly.

Slowly she did so, her eyes going resentfully to his face. There was cold anger there, an anger that was explained as he said contemptuously, 'For your information, I do not steal other people's ideas. Although, being the kind of person you are, I'm hardly surprised that it was the first thought that came into your head—after all, it's obviously the kind of trick that you wouldn't hesitate to carry out,' he finished insultingly.

Purdey rubbed her bruised wrist and retorted, 'The idea is my own!'

'And how did it come to you?'

'It's all in the report—for what it's worth now,' she added bitterly, still convinced that he'd kill it.

But to her surprise he began to go through it with her, taking each point as she'd set it down and asking a great many pertinent questions, and not all of them money-orientated. He seemed to have a wide grasp of all aspects of the hotel trade.

'It's a pity you couldn't have had this idea before we sent the architect over,' he remarked.

'But it was only because Jersey was chosen as a first conference venture that the idea came to me,' Purdey said eagerly, her enthusiasm momentarily overriding her antagonism. 'Jersey is a holiday island, so I thought, why not try to combine the two, so that people going to a conference there would want to

take their families with them? Some of the big
institutions have conferences that last several days,
and companies send their representatives along, so it
would be worth while making it part of the family
holiday. And Jersey is so popular too, because of the
tax and VAT concessions.'

She looked up when Jared didn't speak, and found
his eyes fixed on her, watching her with an abstracted
expression. 'I'm sorry if I'm boring you,' she said
shortly.

His brow flickered and he gave her his attention. 'I
heard what you said.'

Purdey gave him a baleful look. 'All right, so we've
gone through the motions. Shall I go away now so that
you can tear up the report?'

'Why should you think I intend to do that?'

She laughed harshly. 'Because it was my idea, of
course. And you've already said that you intend to get
me fired from this job.' Purdey had got to her feet as
she spoke, and stood before him, tall and slender, her
body thrust forward defiantly.

'And so I do,' Jared answered shortly. He too rose
and came round the desk. 'But my first loyalty and
duty is as a director of this company. And I don't
intend to rob them of the benefit of a good idea
just because it comes from a little cheat like you.'

'You mean—you mean you're going to put it
forward?' Purdey said in disbelief.

He nodded curtly. 'You can send copies to the rest
of the board, and we'll take a decision on it at the next
meeting.'

'I—all right.' Purdey turned to go, still completely
taken aback. She had been so sure that Jared would

thwart her on this.

'Just one moment.' There was something in his voice that made her quickly turn to look at him, afraid again. 'I understand that you've left the hotel. Where are you living?'

'That's none of your business,' she answered shortly.

Jared's eyes narrowed. 'You know, Perdita, you really shouldn't defy me.' His voice was soft, silky—and full of menace. 'I may have to wait, but I shall get what I want eventually.'

'And will it give you satisfaction to ruin me?' she asked on a bitter note. 'With your sense of—of honour, I should have thought you'd be above that.'

'Ah, but you seem to bring out the worst in me,' Jared said mockingly. 'And as for ruining you . . .' His eyes went over her insolently, mentally undressing her. 'I'm quite sure you were—ruined—long ago.'

Purdey's face flamed and she took a hasty step forward, her arm raised to strike him, but she saw the warning glint in Jared's eyes in time and drew back. 'No,' she said venomously. 'You're not worth losing my temper over.' And she strode from the room.

The next week was a very busy one; Purdey sent copies of her report for a leisure centre at the Jersey hotel to the other directors, most of whom found the time to come into her office and discuss it with her from the angle of their own departments and interests, so that at the board meeting they were all fully briefed. That board meeting was a very long one. Purdey was brought in at one point, but there was little she could add to her report. The following day she was called into the managing director's office and told that they wanted her to go to Jersey again to do another feasibility report for the enlarged project in regard to that hotel and that area.

'And we're arranging for the manager of a firm that builds leisure centres, and also an architect and an agent from a Jersey building firm to go along as well. We want as much detail as we can on this before we make a decision,' he told her. 'Basically we like the idea, we think you're right about it being a thing of the future. All we're worried about is whether it's the right thing for that particular hotel. So I'm also sending a director over with you. Probably on the promotion side. I'd like you to go over there in a couple of days' time. Can you manage that?'

'Yes, of course,' Purdey replied promptly. 'I should imagine it will take about a week to prepare a detailed report.'

'Don't rush it,' the managing director warned. 'We want to be absolutely sure before we go ahead with this.' He smiled at her. 'But we very much like the idea, and you had a good advocate in Jared Faulkner; he was very enthusiastic about it.'

Purdey's eyes widened in surprise. 'He was? Why—er—how very kind of him.'

And how unlike him, Purdey thought as she went back to her own office. She tried to think what motive Jared could have for supporting her idea. He must have had some reason; she couldn't imagine him doing anything without thinking the issue out first. Perhaps he thought that she would mess up the whole thing, cost the group a small fortune and be kicked out. In other words, he was giving her enough rope to hang herself. But, if that was the case, why openly associate himself with the leisure centre plan? Purdey worried about it, sure that Jared had some devious plan to disgrace her.

Her thoughts were interrupted by a telephone call from Simon. 'I'm just back from my promotional trip to France,' he told her.

'Oh, really? I heard you went on a sailing holiday.'

He laughed. 'But I promoted the group like mad while I was there. I've just read the report on your leisure centre idea for the Jersey hotel. Sounds great. And I see they're going to send a director with you. How about if I put in for the job? It would be fun to have a couple of weeks in Jersey together.'

'Simon, I'm going there to *work*,' she protested.

'Well, of course. We'll do an hour or so whenever necessary. But I understand there will be a parcel of experts there, so we can let them sort it all out. Simple. All we have to do is deliver their facts and figures when we're ready to come back.'

'You're hopeless. Your work attitude is completely wrong,' she told him.

'Ah, but think what a marvellous attitude I have to life.' She had to laugh at that and he said, 'That's better. And think what a good time we could have away from all the prying eyes. So bring all your glad rags with you, Purdey, and we'll have a good time.'

It was impossible to be mad at Simon, but Purdey put the phone down hoping that he wouldn't be sent to Jersey with her; she wanted to concentrate on the job she had to do, not fight off Simon's advances. But as she prepared to make the trip she heard nothing definite about who was going with her, except that the head of the promotions department was too heavily involved in something else and it was unlikely he could make it. So it seemed that Simon had got his way and they were sending him instead.

Purdey warned her mother and the Gascoynes that she would be away and packed her cases, reluctantly adding several evening outfits. If Simon was going to be there, he was bound to want to go out dining and dancing, and she had an idea that, like a spoilt child, he would pester her until she agreed to go with him.

She was due to fly to Jersey on a scheduled flight from Gatwick airport, and arrived there in plenty of time. At the check-in desk she explained that she was travelling with someone else who would be arriving later, and they reserved the seat next to hers for Simon. Purdey walked through to the less crowded departure lounge and sat down to read a magazine, hoping that Simon would arrive on time. She got absorbed in an article and didn't glance up until someone stood in front of her and said, 'Good morning.'

Her head came up quickly then, for there was no mistaking that cold tone. 'But I thought Simon was . . .' Her voice died as she saw the scorn in Jared's eyes.

'Of course you did,' he said sardonically. 'But I told you to keep away from Simon. And I certainly didn't intend to let you get away with such a useful opportunity to seduce him—all at the company's expense!'

CHAPTER FIVE

PURDEY stared into Jared's triumphant face, and then got to her feet and began to stride towards the exit, but he reached out and put a restraining hand on her arm. 'And just where do you think you're going?' he demanded.

'Certainly not to Jersey with you!' she retorted.

'Suit yourself.' He let go of her arm. 'It will be interesting to hear what the company has to say about your walking away from an assignment.'

She stood still, realising that she couldn't afford to just do as she liked. Not if she wanted to keep her job. Slowly, Purdey turned to look at him. 'I suppose you had this planned from the start,' she said bitterly.

'It had crossed my mind that it might make for—an entertaining few days,' Jared admitted in cold amusement.

'And that's why you were so enthusiastic about it,' she said in sudden realisation. My word, you're devious.'

'Obviously it takes one to know one.' The announcer's voice sounded over the loudspeaker system and he glanced up, listening. 'That's our flight.' He gave her a mocking look. 'Well, are you coming?'

Her face was very pale, but Purdey's chin came up

and she said with equal coldness, 'Of course. I don't give in to browbeating that easily—little as I want your company.'

'And there is of course the fact that you don't have any choice,' Jared reminded her.

As she remembered the debt she owed him, a desolate look came into Purdey's eyes. 'No,' she agreed hollowly, 'I don't.'

He frowned for a moment, but then shook his head as if dismissing some unpleasant thought. 'Let's go.' And he strode towards the embarkation gate.

Purdey followed more slowly so that there were several people between them as they got on to the plane. Quietly she asked the stewardess if she could change her seat, but was told that the plane was full. She moved along the aisle to where Jared waited to let her get into the window-seat, one glance at his face telling her that he'd guessed what she'd done. Averting her face, Purdey slid past him into her seat and kept her eyes fixed on the window until the stewardess came round and told her to do up her safety strap. She did so, awkwardly, aware of Jared watching her. The stewardess began to describe the safety procedures, but after a few moments Purdey looked away, deciding that if it crashed she would be dead anyway. The plane began to taxi along the runway and she slid her hands on to the armrests and gripped hard as it began to take off.

Jared turned to speak to her and then stopped short. 'Are you afraid of flying?' he demanded incredulously.

'I don't know.'

'What do you mean? You either are or you're not.'

'I mean I don't know; I've never flown before.' The plane began to climb and Purdey firmly shut her eyes, convinced the plane was going to drop out of the sky—how could it do otherwise when it was so heavy and there were all these people on board?

Jared said something, but she ignored him until he said, 'It's OK, we've finished climbing. You can open your eyes now.' Purdey did so gingerly, and was enormously relieved to see that the plane was level and the ground was spread like a contour map below them. 'I thought you went to Jersey when you did the conference feasibility study,' Jared remarked.

'I did, but I went by boat.'

'So you didn't spend the money you conned out of me on jet-setting round the world, then?' he said curiously. 'So what *did* you spend it on?'

'That's my business,' she snapped.

'But *my* money. And I would be interested to know just how you squandered it.'

'Squandered it?' She gave a small smile, thinking that he would never have money that was better spent.

'Yes. What did it go on—clothes, a good time for a few months?'

'What makes you think I spent it?'

'Obviously you did. It certainly wasn't a one-off, or you wouldn't be trying to play the same con trick on Simon.'

His disparagement angered her, so, knowing it would annoy him, Purdey said, 'All right. If you must know I spent it all on a trip to America. The whole lot.'

Jared's face hardened. 'I might have guessed. And

you went by boat to try and entrap some rich American, I don't doubt.' He turned away in disgust and opened the briefcase on his knee, took out some papers and started reading them.

They had climbed above the clouds and were in the sun now. Purdey looked out of the window to make sure the wing was still attached to the plane, and thought that maybe flying wasn't so bad after all. She opened her magazine and tried to concentrate on the article she'd been reading. It had absorbed her before, but now she found that it couldn't hold her attention. She kept stealing glances at Jared's hands as he held up a document to read. They were very lean hands, but looked strong and efficient. The nails were square and manicured, the skin soft. Absently he rubbed the back of one, and Purdey could almost imagine him stroking a woman. She wondered if he was married yet, but there was no ring on his hands, not even a signet. He ought to be married, she thought, maybe it would soften him, take away some of that inner ruthlessness. But the next moment Purdey felt a surge of fierce jealousy at the thought of some other woman experiencing his devastating kisses.

The stewardess came round with the drinks trolley. Purdey ordered gin and tonic and drank it down almost in one long swallow. Jared watched her and said in acid amusement, 'For someone in your line of busienss, you have a great many weaknesses.'

'And I suppose you're taking note of every one,' she answered balefully.

'Of course.'

'Well, bully for you. Quite frankly, I couldn't care

less.'

An annoyed frown creased Jared's brow. 'Oh, but you will. I'll make sure of that.'

He went to say something else, but the seat-belt light went on and the plane lurched as it turned to come into land. Purdey grabbed at the armrest, but found Jared's hand already on it so she gripped that instead. He gave an exclamation of surprise, but then turned his hand and held hers, letting her hold on tightly until they were safely on the ground. Only then did she relax and let go. 'Thanks,' she said sincerely, but with heightened colour in her cheeks.

Jared gave a brief nod, and for once didn't make some scathing remark at her expense.

The hotel had sent a car to meet them and drive them the short distance into St Helier; but then, all distances were small on an island that was only ten miles long. Jared gave her half an hour to settle in, and then they did a detailed tour of the hotel and its grounds so that Jared would know the exact layout when they had their first meeting with the architect, builder and leisure centre expert that afternoon.

'Just what did you have in mind?' he asked her.

'Well, as you saw, the hotel already has a small gymnasium which could be used for part of the conference facilities, and instead a new gym could be built into the leisure centre, along with a swimming pool, saunas, a solarium and possibly a jacuzzi. And I thought that the whole leisure complex could be built as an annexe to the hotel to minimise disruption to the guests as far as we possibly can.'

'You propose putting it where this additional car park is?'

'Yes. The manager says it's really only used when there's a big local function on. Most visitors to Jersey don't bring their cars with them; they usually hire one or use local transport. And conference organisers usually provide coaches.'

'Mm. But car parking is important. Possibly we could incorporate some underground parking.'

'Wouldn't that be expensive?'

'Not if it's done at the same time as the complex. They'd have to dig deep for the pool, anyway.' Jared looked around at the hotel grounds with the coast behind. 'That's the area you said they were reclaiming from the sea over on the left there, is it?'

'Yes, and just past it is the harbour and boat marina. But the hotel is within easy walking distance into the town centre, too.'

Jared nodded decisively. 'Yes, it's well-situated.' He glanced at his watch. 'Let's go and have some lunch.'

Purdey didn't relish the idea of having lunch with him, but it turned out to be very much a working meal because the architect and leisure centre expert had arrived by then and Jared spent the time picking their brains. He did it cleverly, by asking about their past experience in this kind of project, and soon had both men talking loquaciously about problems they'd run into in other areas. They bounced ideas off each other too, and Purdey took a pad out of her bag and began to make notes, not wanting to miss anything. Jared glanced at her and his lips curled before he looked away again. OK, so maybe the only notes he made were mental ones, Purdey thought antagonistically, but by writing everything down she was giving him no chance to rebuke her later for forgetting something.

After lunch they went over the hotel again with the two experts and the local builder. Jared immediately took control of the party, which Purdey resented at first, but as she watched the way he handled it her feelings gradually changed to little short of admiration. He certainly knew what he was doing and how to manage the men so that they worked as a team. Purdey knew from her own experience that when you got a group of 'experts' together, they often each wanted to take over and have their own way, so it was instructive to see how Jared manipulated them. Purdey watched and learnt, and didn't object when Jared treated her like a secretary and told her to take notes. 'As you seem so good at it,' he added mendaciously.

Dinner that evening was with the manager of the hotel, who'd been keeping an anxious eye on their activities all day. Again Purdey sat back and let Jared do most of the talking, admiring anew his skill in handling people. The manager became very enthusiastic about the idea, and added a lot of his knowledge about their present clientele to the pool of information Jared was collecting.

The next couple of days were hectic, packed with meetings with the experts and also the various planning and environment departments of the Jersey authorities. And here again Jared's enthusiasm, confidence and knowledge won over people who were initially averse to the development. Thinking about it honestly, Purdey had to admit that she wouldn't have been able to do the job as well as he had. She had the enthusiasm and almost equal knowledge of the project, but against her she had her youth and sex. Disadvantages which any opponents wouldn't have hesitated to use. And she was quite sure that Simon wouldn't have stood a chance. But when Jared entered a meeting, tall and energetic, and with the air of someone who was going to get things done and expected everyone's enthusiastic support, all the opposition seemed not only to melt away but to turn in his favour.

Then came the weekend, when all the official departments were closed. All Purdey had to do that day was to borrow the hotel car and take the two experts to the airport so that they could fly home, their preliminary work done. Now they would be able to liaise in England. Jared had been invited to play a round of golf by one of the local men, and had remarked that it would be a useful place to make contacts. So Purdey had the rest of the day to herself. And it was a most beautiful day, hot and still, with hardly a cloud in the sky. The hotel car was at her disposal until lunchtime, so she took the opportunity to drive round the island, finding it a jewel of a place with breathtaking views over the coastline and rising promontories, each of them crowned with an ancient castle to guard against invasion by the French. Inland there were narrow lanes set between high banks or running between little patchwork fields of crops, with here and there one of the exquisite manor houses for which the island was famous.

Purdey loved the drive, but it soon got very hot in the car and she was glad to go back to the hotel where she changed into a bikini with a loose shirt and wrap-around skirt over it and went down to the beach to sunbathe. It felt great to relax, to just empty her mind and soak up the sun. Almost like being on holiday. She dozed a little, but when she woke her thoughts dwelt on Jared. He was so efficient and capable. As a colleague, she was glad that he was here. She had learnt such a lot from just watching him. But then she froze, realising that Jared was her enemy, and she was quite sure he would have no compunction in turning those qualities against her when he decided that the time was right to get rid of her. Purdey shivered and sat up, feeling suddenly cold despite the heat.

She hadn't eaten yet, and it was almost three o'clock. There were various booths along the sea wall and Purdey turned to look at them, fancying something to eat and willing to be tempted into something fattening in the junk food line. As she looked along her eyes met momentarily those of a rather long-haired young man who was leaning against the wall almost directly behind her. He grinned and nodded, almost as if he knew her. Purdey did a double-take for a moment, but then went quickly on, convinced that he was a stranger. But unfortunately the man's ploy had worked, because he came sauntering over. Purdey groaned inwardly and turned away, but he came up and squatted down on the sand beside her. He was wearing the briefest of bathing trunks, was tanned and muscular, and was obviously hopelessly in love with his own beautiful body. 'Hi,' he said, giving her an 'Aren't you the lucky one?' smile.

Purdey looked at him and yawned.

He blinked at this unexpected reaction, but persevered. 'You here on holiday, doll?'

Ugh! Purdey cringed and said shortly, 'Please go away.'

But the Tarzan clone only gave her a cement-jawed look, let his eyes run over her lasciviously, and said, 'I could fancy you, darlin'.'

With an exasperated sigh, Purdey pulled on her shoes and gathered up her things, knowing that the beach was finished for the day. Getting to her feet, she began to walk away, but he came after her and caught her round the waist, pulling her against him.

'I said I fancied you,' he grated, his eyes angry now.

'Let go of me, you stupid hulk.' Purdey tried to push him away, but he only laughed and held her close to his hips, moving his body against hers.

'Damn you!'

She lifted her arm to hit him in the face, but as she did so caught sight of Jared walking down the beach, watching them. 'Jared! Help me,' she called out.

For a moment she thought that he was going to ignore her, but then Jared came sauntering over, his hands in his pockets, and said, 'Is he annoying you?'

'Yes, he damn well is. Let go of me, you lout.'

Jared turned and looked at the youth. 'You heard the lady.'

The he-man type began to laugh, but then he looked into Jared's eyes and saw the cold, quiet menace there. His laugh died in his throat and he let Purdey go and stepped back, his face sullen. 'It was only a bit of fun. She seemed to like it till you came along,' he said nastily.

Purdey threw him a shrivelling look and would have liked to kill him, sure that Jared would believe him.

When he'd gone she said, 'Thanks,' and began to

pull on her shirt, but not before Jared's eyes had run over her.

'Were you going back to the hotel?'

'Only to get away from that idiot.'

'Stay, then.' And he sat down on the sand, plainly expecting her to do the same.

Slowly Purdey spread her towel and sat down beside him. He was wearing casual, light-coloured trousers and shirt, which made him seem somehow different when she'd only seen him in business suits before. Younger, somehow, and not so unapproachable. She expected him to say something derisory about her luring the youth on, but he didn't. In fact, he didn't seem to have anything to say. He just sat with his elbows on his bent knees, looking towards the sea.

At length Purdey said tentatively, 'How did the game of golf go? Did you win?'

He smiled without humour. 'The other man won the play-off.'

'What does that mean?' Purdey asked, wondering if he was a poor loser.

'Mm? Oh, it means we tied after eighteen holes and had to play another hole to see who won.'

There was something in his expression that made Purdey suddenly realise that he would never stoop to being a bad loser. 'You let him win,' she said intuitively.

Jared's eyebrows rose, but he didn't deny it.

'You're very experienced at—handling people, aren't you?'

He turned his head to look at her. 'You think so, do you?' He shrugged. 'It doesn't pay to antagonise people you want to use.'

'And is that what you do—use people?'

His eyes narrowed as they looked into hers. 'Their expertise, their influence, their goodwill. In business, that's what you need men for.'

'And women?' Purdey couldn't resist asking. 'Do you use women, too?'

He gave a small smile. 'What a very feminine question. Why do you ask it? I wonder.'

'Why don't you answer it?' she countered.

'Do I use women? Don't all men use women to a certain extent? Use their services—in whatever capacity that may be.' And he gave her a mocking look, having evaded a direct answer.

'You ought to be a politician,' she said scathingly.

He grinned suddenly. 'Is that an insult or a compliment?'

Thrown by the grin, Purdey said unsteadily, 'Both, I think.'

In a sudden change of mood, Jared said harshly, 'Well, you should know; you're an expert on using men. Or rather, their emotions. You play on them, don't you? Blowing first hot then cold, until the poor young devils are fast on your line. Crazy about you. Mad for you. But you hold them at arm's length, making promises you don't intend to keep. Why do you do it?' he said in sudden urgency. 'Is it just for the money—or does it amuse you to make men fall in love with you and then make fools of them?'

'I don't make them . . .' Purdey began, but saw the intensity in his face and her voice faded.

'No, you don't have to put yourself out to *make* them fall for you,' Jared mistakenly finished for her.

'With your looks and figure . . .' and his eyes again ran over her '. . . you can't have any trouble finding new dupes. And that air of self-containment, almost of mystery, that you have; it must act as a challenge to any man.'

Purdey hadn't been aware that there was anything at all mysterious about her, and her eyes widened, astonished that he had looked at her with anything but hatred.

'And it's no good giving me that wide-eyed innocent look,' Jared went on harshly. 'You forget that I know you for what you are.'

'Do you?' Her eyes lifted to meet his. 'You're so sure that you're right, aren't you? But then, I'm getting to know you for what you are, too.'

She made to get up, but had only got to her knees when Jared caught her arm. 'And just what do you think I am?' he demanded, his voice smoothly dangerous.

It would be a mistake to tell him, Purdey knew that, but she couldn't stop herself. 'You're cold, ruthless and very cruel,' she said clearly. 'You're completely unable to admit, even to yourself, that you might have made a mistake. You take people at their face value because you don't care enough to find out *why* they're as they are. You're strong yourself, and so you despise weakness in others. I think you're entirely selfish—and quite incapable of ever falling in love.'

Why she added the last she didn't know, but it made Jared's jaw harden and his hand tighten on her arm. 'Quite the analyst, aren't you?' he said harshly. 'But as I don't give a damn what you think of me, it hardly matters.'

But that wasn't true; Purdey had seen and felt his reaction and knew that he wasn't as immune as he pretended. Especially at that last gibe. She frowned, wondering if she had touched a raw spot. Did this man who seemed so strong have a weakness after all?

But she had no time to dwell on the thought because Jared said, 'Before you get carried away by your own cleverness, just remember you still have to answer for what you did. I said I was going to make you pay, and nothing you can do will stop me.'

Purdey gave a small smile. 'You just can't bear to think that you've lost out, can you?' Freeing her arm, she got to her feet and stood looking down at him. 'But you don't have to remind me. I know that you're relentless—another of your charming qualities. No wonder you've never married. No woman in her right mind would . . .'

She broke off abruptly as Jared came quickly to his feet, his eyes glinting with anger. 'Just don't push it,' he said fiercely. 'Or you'll be paying sooner than you think—one way or another.'

Purdey stared at him, only now seeing the danger she was in. She had challenged his manhood, and Jared Faulkner wasn't a man who would ignore a challenge. Dropping her eyes, she stood still and silent until he straightened and stepped back, then she quickly turned and ran up the beach, pausing at the sea wall to put on her skirt before hurrying back to the hotel.

There was to be a band in the dining-room that evening, with dancing until midnight. Even so,

Purdey decided to eat at the hotel because it would be on her expense account. She put on one of her evening outfits, a black lace top and long straight skirt, because she felt that as an executive of the hotel group she ought to look the part even if she was dining alone. She went into the bar first and saw Jared and the hotel manager talking together. Jared had his back to her and she went to walk by, but the manager saw her and stepped forward to meet her. 'Hello, Miss Bruce. What would you like to drink?'

'Oh, that's all right. Please don't let me interrupt.'

But he insisted, and she was forced to join them. He went to the bar to get her drink, and Purdey's chin came up with an air of defiance. She went to say a cold, 'Good evening,' to Jared, but the words died in her throat. He was wearing a dinner-jacket and black bow-tie, and at the sight of him her heart gave a crazy jump, but it wasn't that that took her voice away. He was looking at her so intently, an expression in his eyes that she couldn't fathom, but knew instinctively was from a very deep emotion. His knuckles showed white as he held his glass, and it was a moment before he said in a strange, rasping voice, 'Good evening. You look very lovely tonight.' Purdey blinked, but everything was back to normal as he added, 'Who are you trying to entrap—someone in particular, or will anyone do?'

She was saved from answering as the manager joined them with her drink, but then it was impossible to walk away as she would have liked to have done. The manager, anxious to prove that he was capable of running the much larger hotel that they envisaged, started to tell them of some ideas he'd had, emphasising his local knowledge and giving them what amounted to a hard sell. If she'd been alone, Purdey would have cut him off at the beginning, but letting him talk meant that she didn't have to speak to Jared or even look at him. She was surprised though, that Jared didn't stop him, until it occurred to her that Jared might prefer to listen to the manager than talk to *her*.

But at length even the manager ran out of words, and Jared nodded. 'Very interesting,' he said distantly. 'I'll bear all you've said in mind.' Then he turned to Purdey. 'Let's go into dinner, shall we?'

Putting a firm hand under her elbow, Jared led her towards the dining-room, with the manager walking alongside saying that he'd reserved a special table for them. Purdey half hoped that he would join them, but he excused himself at the entrance and left them in the care of the head waiter, who led them to a table set almost in an alcove on a slightly raised level so that they were overlooking the room, but were screened from most of the other diners. As they approached it, Purdey hung back and said, 'Look, if it's all the same to you, I'd rather eat alone.'

Jared merely said, 'Don't be ridiculous.' The waiter pulled out a chair for her and looked at her expectantly. Caught between them, Purdey had no choice but to take the offered seat.

The waiter left them with the menus and Jared gave her a sardonic look. 'Sorry if I cramp your style, but we've eaten together every other evening so we might as well tonight.'

'The architect and the other man were always with us before,' Purdey pointed out, 'and I regarded them as working meals. But now they're gone and this just happens to be the weekend.'

'What's the matter, Perdita?' Jared taunted. 'Afraid of being alone with me?'

'I can think of a million better ways to spend my time, yes,' she retorted.

He smiled thinly. 'But it will give you an opportunity to tell me all about yourself.'

'And why should you wish to know that?' she asked, immediately suspicious.

'This afternoon you accused me of not bothering to find out why people are as they are. So now I'm going to find out about you,' he replied evenly. 'Isn't that what you want?'

It definitely wasn't. Purdey could think of nothing worse than laying her life bare for this man's scornful inspection. 'And you?' she countered. 'Are you going to tell me all about yourself, too?'

His eyes settled on her. 'For what purpose?'

Her reply was deliberately offhand. 'Oh, it might be amusing to know what has made you as cold and sadistic as you are.'

He gave a small, grim smile. 'Throwing insults already?'

'No, merely trading them.'

'You have no intention of telling me about yourself, have you? What's the matter? Afraid I might find out about your murky past?'

Purdey shot him a fulminating glance and got to her feet, but she was sitting against the wall and had to go past him, and Jared put out his arm, barring her way.

'Sit down,' he ordered.

'Why the hell should I? You have no right to insult

me.'

'No right?' He shot her a venomous glance. 'I have every right. Now sit down and choose what you want to eat.'

Slowly she did so, but Purdey's eyes were still defiant. 'I don't see why I should. The only thing I'm likely to get from a meal with you is indigestion.'

An amused glint came into Jared's eyes for a moment, which surprised her, but he turned his attention to the menu and they didn't speak again until their order had been taken. Then he said, 'Well, are we going to sit in dead silence all evening, or shall we try to find a safe subject to talk about?'

'Dead silence would probably be safer,' Purdey answered wryly.

'Very likely, but very boring. Let's try animals, that should be safe. Do you have any pets?'

'No.' She shook her head. 'How can I when I'm out at work all day and travelling so much? We did have a puppy once, but—but we had to give it away.'

'Oh? Why was that?'

'Our circumstances changed,' Purdey said shortly, remembering how her brother had cried when the poor creature had had to go. But their father had died; they'd had to move from the house to a small flat, Toby was going to a special school and their mother had to go out to work, so there was no way they could keep a dog.

Jared saw the bleakness that came into her face and frowned. '*Our* circumstances?' he questioned. 'Who do you mean?'

But Purdey felt that she'd already given too much away. 'It doesn't matter. What did you think of the manager's suggestions for the hotel?'

'Not enough to discuss them over dinner,' Jared replied promptly. 'Why won't you tell me? Do you have any family?'

'None that I care to discuss with you,' she flashed.

'As sharp as a needle, aren't you? And a needle with a poisoned barb most of the time.'

Purdey flushed slightly. 'One is usually on the defensive against a threat. And as you are continually threatening me . . .'

He gave her a brooding look and then nodded. 'Very well. Why don't *you* think of a safe subject?' He held up a hand. 'But not shop, please. Or we'll both have indigestion,' he said with a smile.

She laughed, and then stopped abruptly, as taken aback by her own laughter as much as his smile. Picking a topic at random, she began to tell him about her tour of the island and found that he knew Jersey quite well, and also a lot about its history, which he told eloquently enough to arouse and hold her interest. That led on to history in general, and from there to art and other subjects, and almost before Purdey knew it the meal was almost over. She could hardly believe that the time had gone so quickly—or so pleasantly. She had actually *enjoyed* sharing a meal with him.

Maybe it had taken him aback, too, because there was a slightly rueful twist to Jared's mouth as he finished his coffee and pushed the cup aside. Some guests were still eating or had left, but most of those who remained were now getting up to dance to the group who played popular music from a low stage set at the end of the room. Jared glanced round at them and then said, 'Would you care to dance?'

Purdey shook her head. 'I don't think so, thanks.'

'Afraid?' he asked, his brow rising mockingly.

'Only that I might get indigestion after all,' Purdey returned coolly.

He smiled at that, and Purdey thought she really had got indigestion, the way her heart lurched. 'I'm willing to risk it,' he offered.

And so Purdey found the unbelievable happening. She walked ahead of him on to the floor and turned to face him, her hands lifting to meet his as he came to stand beside her. It was a slow number and there was no excuse to dance apart. For a moment their eyes met and held, then Jared slowly reached up to take her hand, his other arm going round her waist and drawing her towards him. He danced easily, his body moving in time with the music, but even so Purdey felt that he wasn't relaxed. She sensed a tension in him, possibly because she was tense herself. Somehow it seemed all wrong to be dancing with him, almost a self-betrayal. Her pulses were racing and she was overwhelmed by the closeness, by the sheer bulk of him. The shoulders that she rested a trembling hand on were so broad, and although she was tall herself her eyes were only level with his mouth. Purdey tore her eyes away and looked about the room, but Jared pulled her closer to avoid another couple, and his arm tightened, keeping her against him.

Slowly Purdey lifted wide, uncertain eyes to his face, her breath catching in her throat at what she saw there. His head was half turned away, but his profile was very taut, the planes of his lean cheeks and his jaw sharpened as if he fought some inner struggle. His eyes were half closed and a pulse throbbed at his temple, but he seemed to become aware of her regard and turned to look at her. He didn't say anything. He didn't have to. Purdey saw the dark flame of desire in his eyes and was stunned by it. She stumbled a little and he brought her hand up against his shoulder, his eyes still holding hers, making no secret of how he felt.

Purdey drew in a sharp breath and quickly looked away, her heart racing. That he should want *her*—her of all women. But maybe it wasn't that, maybe he just wanted a woman, any woman. And she was here, forced into his company, alone and vulnerable. Once, she remembered, he had called her a common tramp. Perhaps he still thought her that. She remembered the way he had kissed her so long ago and the way she had responded, and was suddenly afraid. Her voice shaking, Purdey stepped away from him and said, 'I—I'd like to sit down.'

She thought that he was going to reach for her again, but he stopped himself, his brow drawing into a frown. 'Very well,' he said shortly.

They went back to their table and Jared ordered more drinks from the waiter before she could stop him.

'I was going to go up to my room now,' she protested.

'Why? It's early yet.' He put out a hand to stop her picking up her bag, and said in a shocked voice, 'You're trembling!' Quickly she took her hand away and he burst out, 'Damn it, I don't understand you! I *know* you're a liar and a cheat, and yet sometimes . . .' He broke off and took his hand away. 'Go if you want to,' he said shortly.

Purdey hesitated a moment, taken aback, but then walked past him and headed for the nearest exit, double doors that led out on to a terrace overlooking the garden. She was so glad to get away from Jared's disturbing presence that for a few minutes she didn't realise her mistake, but then saw that she had come the wrong way and she would have to go back through the dining-room and out of another door to reach her room. But for the moment it was good to be outside, to feel the slight breeze from the sea on her face and in her hair. She felt hot and agitated, unable to even think straight. And all because of one dance with Jared!

It was only because she hated him so much, Purdey told herself, but knew that it wasn't true. She disliked him, yes, but even so she was strongly attracted to him. An attraction that she couldn't understand.

The roses were out in the garden below, their scent drifting up to her. Purdey went down the steps from the terrace and walked through the gardens until she reached the wall that overlooked the sea. It was a calm night, with a soft silver moon that gleamed on the slow swell of the sea. Waves broke gently on the shore and rippled across the beach, washing it clean. Purdey stood looking down at the scene morosely, wishing that the past could be wiped clean as easily.

Behind her she heard a step on the gravel, but didn't turn round as Jared said, 'Are you all right?'

'Don't tell me you were worried about me,' she answered in self-mockery.

Putting his hand on her shoulder, Jared turned her round to face him. 'You didn't have to run away.'

'Oh, but I did. Dancing with you was a—a mistake.'

'Was it?' Lifting his free hand, Jared ran the back of his fingers down the length of her face, lingering over her lips. 'You're a very beautiful girl,' he said softly.

A pulse began to beat at her throat, but Purdey jerked her head back. 'Does it amuse you to try and seduce me?' she flared at him.

'Is that what I'm doing?'

'You know darn well it is.'

'And am I succeeding?' Jared asked, his eyes intent on her face, his arm slipping down to her waist to pull her close against him.

'No! Not you. *Never.*'

She tried to push him away, but his arm was like a steel band round her, holding her prisoner. 'Who are you trying to convince? Admit you enjoyed dancing with me.'

'*No.*' She broke free of his hold and stood at bay against the wall. 'Is this the way you get your kicks?' she jerked. 'Trying to force someone against their will?'

Anger flashed in Jared's eyes, and he reached out and caught her wrist. 'Damn it,' he bit out, 'you ought to be the last person . . . You witch! You beautiful, bewitching little she-devil.' He pulled her roughly against him. 'I kissed you once before,' he grated, his arms going round her. 'And heaven help me, I've never stopped wanting to do it again.'

There was such raw emotion in his voice that Purdey lifted her head to stare at him in amazement. Could that long ago embrace have had as devastating an effect on him, too? She couldn't believe it. He was too worldly, too sophisticated, to be affected by a single kiss. And yet he had remembered. His closeness was driving her crazy; Purdey could feel the hardness of his body against the length of hers, and she wanted to press herself even closer, a void of emptiness and frustration deep inside consuming her. She shook her head dazedly. 'No. No, I—I don't want this,' she stammered.

'Don't you?' Jared looked down at her, his face in the moonlight silvered into hard, satanic leanness. 'Go, then,' he said, and stepped back, letting her loose.

Purdey stared at him, her body trembling with awareness. Now was her chance, she must take it while she could, but somehow her legs wouldn't move and she couldn't drag her eyes from his face. He waited, a triumphant gleam growing in his eyes, then Jared said softly, 'Come here.'

Some remote inner voice made Purdey shake her head and say, 'No,' but it was a very weak act of defiance, a last feeble attempt for sanity. She took an unsteady step backwards, but came up against the wall. She put her hands on it, gripping the rough surface until her knuckles showed white.

'I said come here,' he repeated, his voice hardening.

Slowly, unable to resist any longer, Purdey pushed herself off the wall and took two immeasurably long paces that brought her close to him. Jared laughed in soft triumph as his arms went round her. But then his face changed, sharpening with desire, as he pulled her roughly against him and bent to take her mouth in the fierce hunger of long-awaited need.

CHAPTER SIX

OH, DEAR heaven. Purdey thought she had remembered so well, but her memories were as nothing compared to the reality of here and now. His kiss was like water to one dying of thirst, like the searing heat of the sun, like the seductive note of a siren's call, like a deep, whirling pool of water in which she gladly sank and drowned. There was no other world, no past and no future, only the reality of his lips, his arms, his closeness, and the overpowering need to be closer still.

Jared tore his lips from hers to rain kisses on her neck, her throat—small, frantic kisses that seared her skin and made her moan in frustrated anguish. He murmured words amid the kisses, words that were a muttered jumble of prayers—or were they curses? He arched her body beneath him, his hand impatiently pushing the black lace aside so that his lips could trace the valley between her breasts. Purdey gasped and gave a little moaning cry as he began to caress her.

He kissed her again avidly, his desire in no way lessened, then stood looking down at her, his breathing ragged, as she leaned limply against him. Her hair shone like molten silver across the darkness of his sleeve, and her mouth was parted, the full softness of her lower lip trembling in awakened desire. The wetness of moonlight-glistened tears clung to the long sweep of her eyelashes, and the soft roundness of her breasts had hardened and lifted the black lace above her pounding heart.

Slowly Purdey opened her eyes, languorously at first, but filling with consternation as she looked into Jared's face. She tried to straighten up, but he held her still. 'I want you,' he said thickly, the words a simple statement of what was to be, an order almost, and again he pushed the lace aside and sought her breast, his hand knowing and expert as he caressed her.

It was the sound of some other people coming into the garden that brought back some degree of sanity. Jared let Purdey go, and for a moment she leaned against the wall, trying to still her quivering body, then turned abruptly and ran back towards the hotel.

'Purdey! Wait.'

Jared's curt command went unheeded as she ran into the dining-room, and hurried through it to the foyer, threading her way through the tables and dancing couples, her heart still pounding wildly, but from the fear of her own susceptibility now. There was a lift with the doors just about to close. Purdey called out, 'Wait—please,' and ran through the gap just in time, the other people in the lift laughing and exclaiming. Her room was on the fourth floor, and luckily she had her key in her bag. Purdey ran down the corridor and into her room like a rabbit scuttling down a hole. She was sure that Jared would come after her, and drew a gasping breath of relief only when the door was closed and securely locked. Then she sat down on the bed and put her

head in her hands. Oh, how could she have been such
a fool? To let Jared even touch her, let alone kiss
her, had been the height of folly. But from that
moment when he had taken her in his arms to dance
with her it had been inevitable. She had lost all power
of resistance; even when she had walked out of the
dining-room some subconscious urge must have sent
her into the garden, knowing that he would come
after her. For a few minutes the memory of the
encounter seared through her brain and she felt
an overwhelming longing to be close to him again.
But to be really close, to have him hold her and love
her, to satisfy this terrible hunger that filled her
soul.

A little moan of despair broke from her, and Purdey
lay down on the bed, curled into a tight ball of
frustration. She grabbed the pillow, filled with a
feeling of helpless rage, and beat her fist against it.
Why of all the men in the world did it have to be
Jared who made her feel like this? Why was it only
he whose kisses set her on fire, and who made her
pride and dislike crumble into nothing when he
touched her? Oh, hell! Was she doomed to spend the
rest of her life longing for a man who only wanted to
subdue and humilate her? To go on loving him in
useless . . . Purdey's thoughts came to an abrupt
halt as she did a double-take. Loving him? Was that it?
Had she been abysmally stupid enough to fall in love
with Jared?

Into the stunned quiet came the sound of purpose-
ful footsteps out in the corridor, and then a sharp
rap on her door. Purdey lay frozen in immobility,
afraid to even breathe. The knock came again, and

Jared's voice, low and determined, 'Open the door, Purdey. I know you're in there.'

But Purdey didn't move or speak, and after a short while Jared went away again. Slowly, then, she got to her feet and slipped off her skirt and top before going into the bathroom to prepare for bed. First she creamed off her make-up, but afterwards stood gazing at her reflection for some time, lost in thought. She felt like a person in shock, punch-drunk almost. And it was no good telling herself that she was wrong, that she couldn't possibly be in love with Jared, because in that moment of self-revelation had come the certainty that it was not only true, but that she would never love anyone else. So what was she going to do about it? Only one solution occurred to her, and it brought a cynical smile to Purdey's lips. Jared had vowed to make her leave the hotel group and he had succeeded, but in an entirely different way from the one he'd intended. But he would never know how or why. He would wake tomorrow and find that she'd left Jersey, left her job, and returned to the oblivion of London, never—if she could possibly avoid it—to see him again.

It was the only way, Purdey was certain of that, much as she disliked the idea. She must run somewhere where he would never find her. Where she would never again feel the temptation of his kiss, because if she did she was lost. He had said he wanted her, and her own body had clamoured for fulfilment. So better to end it now while there was still time, while she still had some few shreds of self-respect left. Turning on the taps, Purdey bent to wash, and then brushed her hair, shaking it loose about her head so that it fell in soft waves to her shoulders. She was wearing only a black teddy, a suspender belt and black stockings when she went back into the bedroom, to be met by the sight of Jared leaning against the door, a key dangling from his hand.

His eyes went over her appreciatively, his lips twisting into a slow smile as he saw the shock in her face.

'How—how did you get in here?' Purdey stammered, her throat so tight she could hardly speak.

For answer, he held up the key. 'Pass key,' he said succinctly, and straightened up. 'I told them that you were feeling unwell and I wanted to check on you. One of the advantages, I find, of being a director of a hotel chain is that the management never argues with you.' He moved towards her as he spoke, a strange glint in his eyes: a mixture of desire and mockery and something else too deep to fathom. He dropped the key into his pocket and lifted a hand to touch her hair. 'Why didn't you let me in?'

'You know why.'

'Because you're afraid?'

'No.' Slowly she raised her eyes to look into his. 'Because I hate you.'

His mouth thinned for a moment, but then he said, 'Maybe you do, at that—but it doesn't stop you wanting to go to bed with me. You want that as much as I do. Don't you?' he asked insistently.

Purdey lowered her eyes, but after a moment said, 'Yes, I want you.'

'Good. I'm glad we've got that settled at last.' Putting his hands on her shoulders he turned her to

face him, then bent to trail his lips slowly up from her
shoulder to her throat, his mouth insinuating and
possessive. She quivered when he bit gently at her
earlobe, and gave a shuddering sigh as his lips found
her breast. But she didn't touch him, her arms hung at
her sides, her hands balled into tight nail-hurting fists.

His mouth was driving her mad, every nerve-end
on fire, and Purdey had to bite her lip to stifle the
moan of pleasure that rose to her throat. But then
Jared straightened so that he could kiss her again
with fierce urgency. She stood still, letting him do
what he wanted, unable to control the trembling of
her body, but taking no active part. His kiss was hard
and passionate, demanding a response, but she gave
him none, not even when he held her against the
growing hardness of his body. But she didn't actively
resist him; that she hadn't the power to do.

Raising his head, Jared looked into her face. He was
breathing heavily and his hair had fallen forward over
his forehead. Tiny beads of perspiration clung to
his brow, his features sharpened by desire. But now
anger grew in his eyes and he said harshly, 'So that's
the way you want to play it. I'm to make all the
running, am I?' She didn't answer and his hands
tightened on her arms. 'Is that the way you get your
kicks; by playing the martyr? The innocent victim?'

'I didn't—I didn't invite you in here,' Purdey
stammered defensively.

'No, but you made it clear you want it. And you're
going to get it,' he rasped curtly. 'And you'll
respond—I'll make darn sure of that, too.'

She tried to pull away from him at that, saying in
sudden fear, 'No. Please go away, I . . .'

But his grip tightened like a vice and he said curtly, 'Oh, no, you don't play those tricks on me. I'm no boy to be played hot and cold with. This time you've gone too far, and there's no going back. You're going to pay the price at last.' His eyes glinted down at her triumphantly, hard and mocking.

Purdey closed her eyes tightly, shutting out that look, trying to shut out the fact that to him this was only a form of revenge. No, not only that. He wanted her, too. The chemistry had worked for both of them. But with Purdey it had gone deep, had pierced her heart, making a wound that would never heal. Slowly she opened her eyes and said huskily, 'Take me, then, if that's what you want.'

A frown flickered between his brows, but then Jared began to kiss and caress her again, and she gave herself up to the wonder and delight of his touch. He knew how to take off a teddy. His fingers searched for and found the two little buttons, undid them and lingered, gently caressing until her body shuddered convulsively and Purdey gasped aloud. He smiled then, and drew the soft silk up over her thighs and over her head, throwing it aside as his eyes explored her lingeringly.

His hands were so sure, so knowledgeable. Purdey couldn't stop herself from crying out as he fondled and caressed her as she stood before him. Almost she raised her arms to hold on to him, but stubbornly resisted the temptation and stood in passive submission, her body on fire with pleasure. Picking her up, Jared carried her to the bed and laid her on it. His face was a taut mask of desire, but there was smouldering anger there too at her refusal to respond.

He undid her stockings and slowly drew them down her legs, his fingers trailing across her skin. Next he took off her suspender belt and stood looking down at her for a few triumphant moments before reaching to undo his tie.

Purdey lay transfixed, unable to take her eyes off him, filled with the strange fancy that as he shed his clothes so he shed the veneers of civility and sophistication, and that underneath there was a man of primitive emotions. Like a wild beast let loose from a cage. As he reached his last garment, Purdey somehow tore her eyes away and lunged across the bed to turn out the lights, plunging the room in darkness.

Jared laughed jeeringly. 'Such modesty!' he mocked.

Going over to the window, he jerked the curtains back so that the moonlight shone in, silvering his lean, strong body. He came over and sat on the edge of the bed, looking down at her. He put an almost casual hand on her breast, but felt her tremble and his grip tightened. His face lost that terrible look of sardonic mockery, became suddenly intense. He seemed about to say something, but Purdey could imagine the disparaging words he would use, and turned her face away from such humiliation.

But strangely, he didn't speak; instead, after a few seconds, he swung himself on to the bed and put his hand under her chin, forcing her head round. 'Look at me, damn you,' he grated. 'This is one game you've lost, and I'm going to make darn sure you know it.' He put his hands on either side of her head and Purdey stared up into his angry face, unable to speak, to fight, to do anything but lie there as he took her in an act that was both primitive and raw in its emotions, but as beautiful as it was wild.

A cloud had slid in front of the moon, plunging the room into darkness when Purdey slipped from the bed a couple of hours later. She groped for her robe and put it on, then hesitated a moment, but finally crossed to the windows and quickly opened them, then stepped out on to the balcony. The night was warm, but it was much cooler out here, a faint breeze coming off the shore to fan her heated body. She leaned against the wall in the angle of the balcony, so that when the moon came out she was hidden in a deep block of shadow. Below, across the gardens, the sea pounded endlessly against the beach, and Purdey would have given a great deal to be able to run down to it and plunge into the sea. To swim out into that silver phosphorescence and cleanse herself in its purifying waters. But it would be impossible to get out of the hotel without being seen, impossible to get out of the room without waking Jared.

She looked through the windows to where he lay asleep, one arm flung out across the bed as if reaching for her. As he had reached for her the second time, Purdey remembered, and tears came to her eyes and fell softly on her cheeks. It had been such exquisite torture that second time. The first savage hunger was spent, and Jared had deliberately set out to seduce her, to make her forget everything but the ecstasy of love as he caressed her with hands and lips and body. He had vowed that he would make her respond, and she had almost succumbed a dozen times, wanting to hold him close, to give as well as take. She had wanted to touch him in return, to feel his body quiver with pleasure like hers, and to tell him that she loved him. But theirs had been a silent coupling, there had been no words of love or even need. She had cried out more than once, and Jared had groaned long and shudderingly as he had reached the peak of excitement, but there had been no words, no tender endearments. And afterwards he had rolled away and they had lain apart—united in the closest bond of all and yet totally divided by prejudice.

And it was this that had kept her quiescent, had made her a tool for his lovemaking. She had reacted, she couldn't help it, her body writhing as Jared lifted her to the heights of pleasure, her head tossing from side to side as she gasped and moaned. But even then she hadn't touched him, her hands clutching the sheets as her body arched and trembled. And afterwards, when Jared could no longer hold back his own excitement, Purdey had turned her head away and lain rigidly still until he had given an angry exclamation and moved away.

It should have been so good, so wonderful, Purdey thought as the tears fell faster. Physically, she supposed, it had been more than good, but it had been joyless. Without love, how could it be otherwise? And she had been too afraid to let him see how she felt. For she was sure that Jared would take her love and use it against her. Use it and defile it. So she had defended herself with the only weapon she had: passionless, unresponsive detachment.

The sound of the door opening made her turn quickly and see Jared come through on to the balcony. He was quite naked and quite unconcerned about it.

Purdey lifted a hasty hand to wipe away the tears, but Jared caught her hand and pulled her out into the moonlight where he could see her face. 'Tears?' he questioned frowningly.

Her head came up. 'Certainly not.'

He looked at her for a moment, then said heavily, 'Why didn't you tell me that you were so—inexperienced?'

'Would you have believed me?'

'Probably not,' he agreed after a long pause.

'Well, then.' And she looked away.

'You must have been very clever,' Jared said musingly. 'Holding the men you've conned at arm's length for this long.'

'I'm not going to apologise for my inexperience, if that's what you're getting at,' she retorted sharply.

'Damn you, it isn't.' Taking hold of her arm, Jared turned her to face him. 'Why are you like this? What have you got against men to use them and hate them?'

'I don't hate *men*—I just hate *you*!'

'Because you're a poor loser,' he sneered.

Suddenly angry, she said bitingly, 'Because I'd rather have given myself to that Rambo clone on the beach than you!'

'You little liar. You can't bear to admit that you're beaten. And too much of a miser to give anything of yourself away.'

'Not to you, at any rate. No way!' Purdey burst out in a flame of resentment.

'No? Well, we'll have to see about that, won't we?' Jared shot back menacingly, his anger aroused.

'No.' Too late Purdey saw where her defiance had led her. But Jared had already pushed the robe aside.

His hands slid inside as he began to caress her, and soon she closed her eyes and let him arch her body towards his, slim and beautiful in the moonlight.

His lips caressed her, too, and she felt the growing hardness of his body. 'This time,' he said. 'This time.' And he picked her up and carried her back into the bedroom.

Almost, he won. As her quivering body reached a height of climactic excitement, Purdey reached out and put her hands on his shoulders, her nails digging into his flesh. But it was only for a moment, and then she snatched them quickly away with a choking cry.

He let her alone then and they both fell asleep, but when Purdey woke early in the morning the space beside her was empty. He had dressed and gone.

Purdey lay awake watching the room gradually lighten and sunlight filter in. Her body felt bruised, but not as battered as her mind. She felt as if her life had come to a sudden barrier, and ahead lay only blackness with no light to show her which way to go, what step to take. There was only one thing she was sure of; that there was no way she wanted to see Jared again today. She got up quickly and had a bath, dressed and collected a towel and swimsuit, then left the hotel to walk along the coast road until a bus came along and took her to a beach on the other side of the island. She stayed there all day, sunbathing and catching up on her lost sleep. At some point in the early evening she had a meal that she prolonged as much as she could by drinking several cups of coffee afterwards, so it was quite late by the time she finally went back to the hotel in St Helier. She did so with the fixed determination to resist Jared in the future.

Last night had proved that love on her side wasn't enough. With Jared feeling only contempt for her, the physical act of love, exciting as it had been, had turned to dust and ashes, had become a barrier instead of bringing them closer.

She had prepared herself to resist his coercion, so it came as something of an anticlimax when Purdey got back to the hotel and there was no sign of Jared. She went to the desk to collect her key, and the receptionist handed her a telephone message from Simon. Purdey took it and said, 'Will you please make sure that no calls are put through to my room tonight?'

The receptionist said he'd see to it right away, and Purdey went nervously up to her room, half expecting to see Jared at any moment. But she reached her room without mishap, then stood outside the door, remembering that last night Jared had used a pass key, and afraid to go in in case he was waiting for her. But not knowing was worse than knowing, so she resolutely turned the key and went inside. The room was empty. Purdey gave a gasp of relief and hurriedly grabbed up a chair and wedged it against the door so that Jared couldn't get in even with a key.

She undressed and showered, but as she came back into the bedroom the phone began to ring. There was only one person who had the power to override her instructions to the receptionist. Purdey let it ring several times, then slowly walked across and picked up the receiver.

'Purdey?' She didn't answer, and Jared said, 'I want to see you. Come down to the bar.'

But she reached out and depressed the rest, cutting him off, then left the receiver lying beside the phone.

For at least half an hour Purdey sat on top of the bed, half expecting him to knock or to try the pass key again, but he didn't and she eventually got into bed and turned out the lights.

The next morning there was to be a meeting with a man from the planning department of the States Council at ten o'clock. It was basically a preliminary meeting to outline their ideas for the expansion of the hotel and prove that it wouldn't harm the local environment. Purdey had breakfast sent up to her room and didn't go downstairs until five minutes before the meeting was due to start. She put on rather a severe grey dress with a white collar and cuffs, and a wide grey leather belt that emphasised the slimness of her waist. Her hair she brushed up into a pleat at the back of her head.

The man from the States of Jersey council had already arrived and brought two companions with him. As Purdey walked into the foyer she saw the manager introducing them to Jared. Without hesitation, she walked up to join the group.

The manager saw her first. He smiled at her, but it was a different smile than any he had used before, and Purdey was instinctively aware that he knew that Jared had spent a night with her. 'Good morning, Miss Bruce,' he greeted her. 'I hope you've recovered from your—er—indisposition.'

She inclined her head. 'Yes, thank you.'

'My colleague, Perdita Bruce,' Jared said from her left. And he introduced the three men. 'Perhaps we should start by taking a look at the area we want to extend over,' he suggested, and ushered the way towards the door. But once outside he fell into step beside Purdey. 'Good morning,' he said shortly.

She hardly glanced at him as she returned the greeting.

'Where did you go yesterday?'

'Sunbathing.'

They reached the secondary car park, and she deliberately turned away from Jared to speak to one of the local men to ask him what were his particular interests in the project, smiling at the man as she did so. Jared watched her for a moment, a brooding look in his eyes, and didn't turn away until his attention was attracted by one of the other men.

The meeting went on for some time, and Jared invited the men to lunch at the hotel. Purdey automatically joined them, but took care not to sit next to Jared. During the course of the meal, though, it was impossible to avoid his eyes completely, and she was startled by the intensity of emotion that she saw there. She took it for anger because she'd stayed away from the hotel yesterday and hadn't obeyed his instructions to meet him in the bar last night.

After lunch, Jared went to the entrance to see the men off, while Purdey went into the small room they'd been using as an office. There she put a call through to Simon in England. 'You're a very elusive lady,' he told her. 'Why haven't you returned my calls?'

'I've been very busy,' Purdey evaded. 'Lots of meetings and things.' She carried the phone over to the window and sat on the window-seat, her back against the wall.

'I've missed you. When are you coming home?'

'Within a couple of days, I should think. There's

not a lot more that can be done here until the architect has drawn up his plans.'

'Will you come out with me when you get back?'

'I don't know.'

'Don't you like me, Purdey? Is that it?'

'You know I do,' she replied reluctantly. 'But Simon, you know how difficult it is. The directors . . .'

'To hell with the directors!' he cut in fiercely. 'I'm not going to let them interfere in our lives.'

She laughed. 'Caveman stuff, huh?' She heard a slight noise and turned her head to find Jared watching her. She hadn't heard him come into the room, and had no idea how long he had been there listening. 'Simon, I have to go now.'

'You promise to let me know when you're coming back to England?'

'Yes, I promise.'

'Good. Well, hurry back. I'm missing you.' She almost put the phone down, but lifted it again as she heard him say, 'Oh, by the way, that friend of yours from way back that you mentioned; I ran into him at the weekend. You know, Alex Nash.'

Purdey caught her breath and felt Jared look at her sharply. 'Oh, did you?' she managed hollowly.

'Yes,' Simon replied cheerfully. 'I told him I'd met you and he remembered you straight away.'

Turning her back on Jared, she lowered her voice. 'Oh, Simon, you shouldn't have done that. What—what did he say?'

'The same as you really; that you used to know each other years ago.'

'I see.' Purdey would have liked to ask a lot more, but was acutely aware of Jared behind her. 'Well, goodbye, Simon. See you.'

She replaced the receiver and got quickly to her feet, walked over to the desk and put the phone back, then turned as if to make for the door, but Jared said curtly, 'I take it that was Simon Gascoyne?'

'Yes.' Purdey stopped, but kept her face turned away.

'I told you to keep away from him.'

'I know what you told me.'

Coming round the desk, Jared took hold of her shoulder and made her turn round to face him. His face was very tense, his eyes cold. 'Why did you avoid me yesterday?'

She gave a high-pitched laugh. 'I should have thought that was obvious. I wanted to get away from you—and as far as possible.'

'That was the action of a hysterical teenager,' Jared shot at her. 'If you'd come down to the bar we could have talked things over and . . .'

'There was nothing to talk over,' Purdey interjected fiercely. 'Unfortunately it happened, and now it's over.'

'Over?' he questioned, his eyes narrowing.

'Yes. Because it's a——' she groped for a word '—an experiment I don't care to repeat.'

Jared gave a short laugh. 'Who are you trying to convince—me or yourself?'

'I hate you!' Purdey exclaimed, inflamed by his mockery.

'No, you don't.' He put his free hand on her other arm, his eyes darkening as he looked down into her face. 'You just hate the way I make you feel. It makes you vulnerable, and you've never felt that way before.

That's what you resent.'

As he spoke he drew her towards him, but Purdey put up her hands to hold him off. 'No, it's you I resent. You I hate.'

But Jared just laughed and jerked her forward so that she was leaning against his chest. Then his arms went round her and he kissed her hungrily.

It might have been a second, or a minute, or an hour; Purdey had lost all sense of time when there came a sharp rap on the door and the manager marched in. 'Oh, I beg your pardon,' he exclaimed. 'I didn't realise. I'll come back some other time.'

But Jared had let Purdey go and she walked across to the window, her face flaming, and knowing full well that for all his feigned surprise the manager had been expecting—perhaps hoping—to catch them in a compromising situation.

'You wanted something?' Jared said curtly.

'Yes, this telex came for you.'

'Thank you.' Jared read it quickly, then said, 'There won't be any reply.'

'Right. I'll—er—leave you to it, then.' And the odious man went away at last.

Purdey turned to follow him, but Jared said, 'Where are you going?'

'To my room, of course.'

'No, you're not, we've got work to do. Can you use a word processor?'

'Yes.' Purdey nodded and turned reluctantly.

'Let's get to work, then. I want a précis of all we've done and learnt here ready to present at the board meeting on Wednesday. But first you can book us two seats on the first plane to London tomorrow.'

Purdey sat down at the desk to do so, and after she'd made the reservation Jared came up behind her and put a hand on her shoulder. 'I'm sorry he came in and saw us.'

His hand felt infinitely comforting, and Purdey had to fight a strong urge to cover it with her own. Instead she said coldly, 'It hardly matters. It only confirmed what he already suspected.'

'How do you know?'

She shrugged. 'Call it feminine intuition.' But then she added on a spurt of anger, 'I could tell by the way he looked at me, stripping me with his eyes. He hadn't dared to do that before because he thought I had some standing in the group, but now he thinks that I'm just here as your—your . . .' Her voiced faded and she couldn't go on.

Jared's hand tightened and he said, 'Purdey, 'I . . .'

But she jerked away from him. 'You said we had some work to do, didn't you?'

He gazed down at her bent head for a moment, his lips drawn into a thin line, then he, too, became businesslike and they spent the next few hours working on a detailed report. They worked well together, but it was impossible to dispel the tension between them completely, and Purdey gave a sigh of relief when the report was finished at last. She stood up and said, 'I'll go and put a duplicate copy in the post to head office, just in case.'

'All right. Then we'll change and have dinner.'

'No.' Purdey turned to face him, her eyes vulnerable but determined. 'I don't want to.'

'Because of the manager? You don't have to be afraid of him. If he makes trouble for us, I'll get rid of him.'

'How powerful you sound,' she said derisively. 'You always get your own way, don't you? Have everything that you want?'

'Not everything, no.' He gave her an odd look. 'Perhaps not even what's becoming the most important thing.'

Purdey shook her head, not understanding. 'I'm going up to my room. I'll see you when we leave for the airport in the morning.'

'Perdita, I would like to talk to you,' Jared said earnestly.

She turned at the door, surprised at his tone, then shook her head. 'We have nothing to say to each other.'

'You're wrong; we have a great deal to say, if only you would listen.'

But again she shook her head and walked out of the room.

Their flight back to England was a one-class only, and they had to share the row with another passenger so there was no opportunity to speak of personal things, for which Purdey was grateful. And when they reached Gatwick Simon was waiting there for them. She had phoned him, as she'd promised, to let him know that she was coming back today, but had no idea that he would come to meet her. But, as they came out of Customs into the main concourse, he waved and strolled up to them. 'Hello. Had a good flight?'

'We got here,' Jared answered sardonically, and threw Purdey a fulminating glance, evidently convinced that she had arranged this.

There was little point in trying to convince him

otherwise; Purdey just said, 'Hello, Simon,' and stepped back when it looked as if he might kiss her.

'I was round this way, so I thought I'd offer you both a lift back to the office,' Simon explained.

Neither of them believed him; Jared certainly didn't. 'How opportune,' he remarked drily. 'However, I have my own car here.' He looked at Purdey. 'And you?'

She shook her head. 'No, my car is being serviced. I came by train.' She gave Simon a brilliant smile. 'So I'd be glad of a lift. Thanks.'

'You'll need this, then,' Jared said, and took her case from the trolley to hand to Simon. He turned to her, his face a cold, withdrawn mask. 'I'll let you know what the board think of our report after the meeting tomorrow.'

'You're not coming back to the office?'

'No, I'm going back to my own office—in London.' Then Jared gave them both a curt nod, picked up his own case and strode away without a backward glance.

They watched him go, and Simon said, 'What's got into him? I thought he was going to the hotel group office.'

'Evidently he changed his mind.' She turned and said rather irritably, 'Let's go.'

Simon's car was right outside and they were soon on their way, but Purdey sat silently until Simon glanced at her and said, 'You're mad at me for coming to meet you. Right?'

'You knew Jared would be there.'

'Jared's all right. He isn't like the other old fossils on the board.'

'But you're wrong,' Purdey told him. 'It was Jared

who told me to keep away from you.' She gave a wry smile. 'He's afraid I might corrupt you.'

'Is he now?' Simon gave a whistle of astonishment. Then he gave her a sidelong glance and said, 'I'm quite willing to be corrupted, you know.'

She gave a rueful laugh. 'You know something, Simon—one day you're going to meet a girl who's going to get really angry with you. And when you do, hang on to her, because you'll know that she really loves you.'

'But you're not that girl?'

'No.'

'That's a pity.' He negotiated a turning and said, 'Is there someone else, Purdey, someone you get angry with?'

She hesitated a moment, then said, 'Yes, there is.'

'Thought there might be. But I take it that true love isn't running smoothly?'

'Not only not running smoothly, not running at all,' Purdey agreed with a harsh, painful laugh.

'Is there anything I can do to help?'

She turned her head to look at him, then reached out to touch his arm. 'Thanks, Simon, but there's nothing anyone can do.'

He glanced at her, seemed about to say something, then changed his mind, and they drove in silence the rest of the way to the office.

As Jared had promised, he came to tell her the results of the board meeting just after lunch on the following day. Purdey had taken her sandwiches to eat outside as it was a fine day, and she was sitting on one of the garden seats, gazing out across the grounds when he came to find her.

'May I join you?'

Purdey looked up and gave a half-nod, then lowered her gaze to the gardens again.

'The board have decided to go ahead with the leisure centre at the Jersey hotel,' Jared said shortly, after he'd sat down. 'They've agreed with all our recommendations, and they've also decided to look into adding leisure and conference facilities to two hotels in England. One of them is to be here, and they want you to select the other.'

'Me? Not the projects manager?'

'No. They feel that this is your baby and you should see it through.'

That they should give her the job was a great achievement, Purdey was fully aware of that, but somehow she felt no sense of elation or even satisfaction. It was a pyrrhic victory, and left only a dry taste in her mouth.

'You'll take the job?'

She nodded mechanically. 'Yes, I suppose so.'

Jared turned to study her averted profile. His voice heavy, he said, 'Purdey, there's something I have to ask you. Are you—serious about Simon?'

It was an unexpected question, but she was more interested in what lay behind it. She turned to look at him for a moment, but could read nothing in his expression, so got to her feet and walked the few steps to where a bed of roses grew. 'Why do you ask?'

'Because I want to know.'

Purdey smiled slightly and bent to smell one of the roses. She might have known she'd get nothing out of him. Straightening up, she turned to face him and said with bitter irony, 'No, I'm not serious about him.

You won't have to buy me off this time.'

'Good. I'm glad.'

'Why? Because you'll save your money?'

'No.' Jared came to stand beside her, his eyes fixed intently on her face. 'Because I want to go to bed with you again.' Fire flashed in Purdey's eyes as she went to walk away, but Jared stepped in front of her. 'And because I'm beginning to think that maybe I was wrong about you.'

Her head came up at that and she stared at him. 'What—what do you mean?' she managed through a throat gone suddenly dry.

Lifting his hands, Jared put them on her arms. 'Nothing that I've learned about you is consistent with the type of person who would steal and cheat,' he said slowly. 'It's like looking into a distorted mirror; I don't see what I expect to see. You're too intelligent and clean, and—and innocent to be all the things I thought you.' He paused and lifted a hand to run a finger along the line of her jaw. 'But the fact remains that you *did* take that money. Why, Purdey?' he said in sudden urgency. 'You *must* tell me why you took it.'

Her heart had begun to race, filled with an almost unbelievable flicker of hope as Purdey gazed up into his intent face. 'Yes, there—there was a reason,' she stammered. 'I needed the money. I had to take it. You see, I . . .'

She broke off as she saw that Jared had lifted his head and was gazing past her. She felt him stiffen, grow rigid, and she swung round to see what had caused it. Two men were walking down the path leading from the hotel towards them. One of them was

Simon. And the other . . . Purdey gasped and stared.

Simon lifted a hand and called out, 'I knew I could help, Purdey. Look, I've found him for you. Here's Alex!'

CHAPTER SEVEN

AFTER that first stunned moment, Purdey swung round to Jared and said urgently, 'I didn't know. I don't . . .'

But Jared's hands bit into her arms and he said savagely, 'So the mirror wasn't distorted, after all. You *are* everything I ever thought you!' And he pushed her roughly aside, turned on his heel and strode away.

Purdey watched him go, her heart filled with a hopelessness that was far worse than before. To have been lifted so high and dashed so low; it was hardly bearable.

'Purdey? Well, aren't you going to say hello to him?' Simon called.

She turned slowly, her eyes bleak, and had to make a tremendous effort to greet Alex. 'Hello, Alex. How are you?'

'Fine. And you?'

'Yes. Fine.' There had been a guarded note in Alex's voice, and she slowly remembered that she had abandoned him without saying goodbye or leaving any word of explanation. It had seemed a terrible thing to be made to do at the time, and she could imagine how hurt Alex must have felt, but right now she couldn't feel anything beyond a profound sense of loss and despair. 'Simon tells me you've been abroad,' she managed.

'Yes, in Canada and Australia mostly. Learning farming and estate management.'

'That sounds very interesting. Did you enjoy it?' Polite small talk, that veneer of sociability that saved you from really having to listen or from giving anything of your inner self away, was all Purdey could think of at the moment.

But Simon wasn't having that. Before Alex could answer, he intervened indignantly. 'I don't believe it. You two have been apart, how long is it? About four years? And all you can do when you meet is talk about farming. I wash my hands of you.'

'Simon,' Alex put in firmly, 'get lost.'

'Huh, the story of my life. Oh, I'm going.' But first Simon bent to kiss Purdey on the cheek and murmured, 'I *said* I wanted to help. Hope things start to flow more smoothly now.' Then he lifted a hand in casual salute and left them alone.

So that was why he'd brought Alex here; he'd thought she was pining for him when she'd wanted Jared. Purdey's mouth twisted ruefully as she turned back to Alex.

'I hope you're not angry that Simon brought me here,' he said stiffly, the hurt pride raw in his voice.

'No, of course not. I'm glad to see you. But . . .'

'He said you would be—although I can't understand why when you went off like you did.'

'Alex . . .' She hesitated, then went on, 'Look, I'd like to put things right between us but—perhaps Simon didn't explain—I work here for the hotel group.' And she indicated the dower house with a wave of her hand.

'Yes, he told me.'

'Well, this is my lunch hour and I ought to be getting back.'

'I see.' Alex drew his shoulders back stiffly.

'No, you don't. I meant what I said about putting things right. Look, can you hang around until I've finished work? Wait at the hotel or something? I'll get away as early as I can.'

'Yes, I suppose so.' He nodded. 'All right, I'll be up at the hotel with Simon.

'Thanks, Alex. I'll see you there. And—and thanks for coming to see me.' Quickly she hurried back through the gardens to the dower house, and was just in time to see Jared driving away, gravel flying up from his tyres as he accelerated down the drive.

The afternoon seemed to drag by as Purdey continually wondered what might have happened if Alex hadn't come along. If she'd had a chance to tell Jared the truth he might have . . . Might have what? Forgiven her? And if he had . . . But that was a fantasy world, and she tried to shut it out. Happiness was as far away from her as it had ever been. And in the meantime she had her coming meeting with Alex to worry about.

The first thing he would want would be an explanation, and she realised that she would have to think up an excuse, because there was no way she could tell him the truth. Well, she would think of something to tell him. But then what? It worried her that he had been so quick to come down here with Simon, and she hoped he didn't still fancy himself in love with her. They had been so young then. His feelings must have changed by now. He must have met lots of other girls while he was abroad.

It was just after four-thirty when Purdey managed to leave the office. As she walked over to the hotel she was confident that Alex had only come to see her so that his youthful hurt pride could be assuaged. He just *had* to know why she'd run out on him, that was all. And, once she'd given him an excuse that would appease him, he would go away satisfied and she would never see him again.

And that would make Jared happy, if nothing else, she thought bitterly. She came to the spot where they had stood that afternoon, and paused, filled with desolation. Now she would never know how he felt about her. Had he too fallen in love? Or did he just want to have an affair, and was seeking to appease his conscience by whitening her blackened reputation? Purdey's lips twisted into a grim smile. The latter, most probably, knowing Jared. After all, the only definite thing he had ever said was that he wanted to go to bed with her again. And it was hard to imagine Jared in love. Would he go into it with the energy and skill that he gave to all his other undertakings? Or would it turn him into something approaching a human being for once?

Her steps slower, she went on towards the hotel, and when she reached it she saw Alex waiting for her on the wide stone steps. She had phoned ahead to say she was coming and he must have got rid of Simon again. Her feelings weren't so chaotic now and she was able to look at him properly. He looked older. Four years ago his face had had the innocence of youth, but now it had the lean, hard lines of a man. His hair had been bleached a couple of shades lighter by the sun, and his shoulders and chest seemed to be a whole lot broader than she remembered.

'Where's Simon?' she asked as she came up.

'He pushed off.' Alex came down the steps to meet her, his hands thrust into his pockets. 'What would you like to do? Have tea at the hotel, or go for a walk or a drive?'

'You look as if you're more used to an outdoor life now.' She glanced around her and decided she didn't want to stay near the hotel. 'It's a lovely afternoon; why don't we go for a drive?'

'OK. My car's over there.'

He had a white sports coupé with the hood off. Purdey got in the passenger seat, and as they drove away reached up to unpin her hair and let the wind blow it into a halo around her head. They drove for about half an hour, the road gradually climbing until they reached the highest point of a range of hills. Alex parked the car and they got out and walked along a path through a grove of trees that led to a piece of open ground with magnificent views over the surrounding countryside.

Looking around appreciatively, Alex sighed and said, 'It's good to be home.'

'Did you dislike being abroad?'

'No, not really. It was all right—after a while.'

He said the last words heavily, after a deliberate pause, and Purdey realised what he was referring to. She said slowly, 'I suppose you wondered why I—I moved away and didn't contact you.'

'The thought did cross my mind once or twice,' he agreed on a sardonic note.

Purdey gave him a quick glance, recognising an

aspect of Jared in his tone. But physically there was little resemblance, and she was somehow glad about that. Keeping as near to the truth as she could, Purdey said, 'I lost my job at the nightclub, so I couldn't afford to go on living in my digs. I had to leave.'

'That was hardly reason enough for you not to even phone to tell me,' Alex pointed out in remembered hurt. 'Where did you go?'

'To live with my family. But—but there was a problem, some family trouble.'

Alex looked at her enquiringly, but when she didn't go on said harshly, 'The same thing still applies; why couldn't you pick up the phone and explain?'

'Because it was a private matter. We didn't want anyone else to be—be involved.'

'I see,' Alex said shortly. He strode forward a few steps and sat down on the grass, his face angry.

'No, you don't,' Purdey said, coming to sit beside him. 'And I'm sorry, but I can't explain any further. You'll just have to accept my word for it that I had to go away and not contact you. It was for the best, Alex, really.'

'Was it? I would have liked to be my own judge of that.' He paused, then said abruptly, 'Did you meet someone else?'

'No, Alex, honestly.' After hesitating a moment, Purdey added, 'It was my brother, he was very ill.'

'Oh, I'm sorry.' There was immediate sympathy in his tone. 'But surely . . .' He broke off. 'Can't you tell me about it?'

'Maybe one day. Not now.'

He sighed, then shrugged. 'All right. But I—I

missed you like hell, Purdey.'

'And I you. I'm sorry.'

They were silent for a few moments, then Alex said with a raw laugh, 'Do you remember that you said you'd marry me if I was still in love with you when I was twenty-five?'

'Did I? It seems a lifetime ago.'

'It seemed like a lifetime before I would be twenty-five when you said it. But I will be twenty-five in a couple of months. Ironic, isn't it? As a matter of fact, that's why I came home. I officially take over my inheritance on my birthday.'

She gave him a surprised look. 'Your grandfather has died?'

'Yes, a couple of years ago.' He gave a rueful grin. 'He always thought I was too young and headstrong, so he made a proviso that I had to wait until I'd learned some sense—his words—before I came into any money.'

'And have you?' Purdey asked teasingly.

'Well, I'm more experienced than I was,' he admitted.

'Tell me about it,' she invited. 'Tell me all that you've done these last four years.'

Alex looked at her for a moment, then rolled over on to his stomach and began to talk. It took quite some time to recount his experiences, because he threw in lots of anecdotes that made Purdey laugh delightedly. His eyes dwelt on her as she lay beside him on the grass, and grew warm when she laughed. When he'd finished he demanded that she tell him all that had happened to her while he'd been away, but he did so guardedly, afraid that she would hold back.

Purdey smiled and reached out to turn his wrist over to look at his watch. 'The pubs will be open. Why don't we find one so that I can tell you over a drink? You must be thirsty, too.'

So they drove to a pub where they sat outside in the sun and drank tall glasses of cool beer. Alex was stunned when she told him about her college degree and the position she'd reached in the hotel group.

'When Simon said you were working for his company, I thought he meant as a typist or something,' he admitted. He looked at her with dawning respect that changed to a slight frown. 'I suppose you're a dedicated career woman now?'

'It looks that way,' Purdey agreed lightly. 'I certainly enjoy my work. And I get to travel around the country quite a bit too, which is a bonus.'

'I've had enough of travelling,' Alex said feelingly. 'All I want to do is to settle down in one place.' He hesitated. 'You know, I tried to find you after you disappeared, but I didn't have much time to look; my grandfather arranged for me to go out to Canada almost at the same time as you—you left London.'

'I see.' Rather at a loss, Purdey said hastily, 'I'm hungry. Tell you what, you were always buying me meals, now it's my turn to buy you one.'

'I can't let you do that,' Alex objected.

She laughed. 'Don't worry, I didn't mean the Ritz, only here at the pub.'

So they ate and began to pick up the threads of their old friendship. Purdey found that Alex hadn't lost his open nature and she still liked him, but that was as far as it went, as far as it would ever go now. But there was a lot to talk about, a lot to catch up on, and it was dark when Alex drove her back to the office to collect her car. He saw her over to it and said, 'I've enjoyed this evening, Purdey. I'd like to see you again.'

'Well, I expect we'll run into each other,' she answered lightly, trying to fob him off.

But he was persistent and said, 'No, I mean that I'd like to take you out. Some time soon. Perhaps we could go to the theatre; I've got a lot of shows to catch up on.'

'That's kind of you, Alex, but . . . Look, I don't know if you're aware of it, but your uncle is a director of the hotel group.'

'Jared? Yes, I know. It was him you were talking to when I came along this afternoon, wasn't it?'

'Yes. And I'm pretty sure that he—he wouldn't approve of me going out with you.'

'Why ever not? What has it got to do with him?'

A hell of a lot, if you only knew, Purdey thought wryly, but just said, 'Well, I sort of work for him. He wouldn't want an employee going out with his nephew.'

Alex burst into laughter. 'He isn't that old-fashioned. And anyway, what he feels doesn't come into it.'

'Doesn't it?'

'No. I'll decide for myself who I want to go out with.'

She smiled. 'You've grown up.'

'I hope so. Will you come out with me?' And he added awkwardly, 'I've lost touch with most of the crowd I used to go around with.'

'Aah,' she mocked, which made him grin. But then she shook her head. 'I'm sorry, Alex, but it will make

Jared too angry.'

His eyes frowned in surprise. 'Why are you worrying about Jared? It has nothing to do with him.'

'But I have to work with him,' she pointed out.

Alex argued, she resisted, but he proved to be far more persistent than she'd expected. Having got her address from Simon, he turned up at the cottage a couple of evenings later and insisted on taking her out for a meal, because he owed it to her, he said. And although they'd made no date he came again on the Saturday, announced that he had two tickets for the theatre and drove her up to London to see the show.

Purdey hadn't minded going out to dinner locally because the chances of Jared finding out were remote, but the whole time they were in London she kept looking over her shoulder, afraid that he might be somewhere near. It wasn't until they were having supper afterwards that Alex happened to remark that Jared had gone to America on business for a couple of weeks, and Purdey relaxed with a groan. 'Why didn't you tell me before? I've been on tenterhooks in case he saw us together.'

'You've got a fixation about Jared,' Alex told her. 'Is he such an ogre at work?'

'No, I . . . I'm just afraid of losing my job, that's all.' She looked at Alex's raised eyebrows and said lamely, 'Jared has a lot of influence with the board. When I took up the position, I said that I had no ties and would be free to travel. If he thought that I was going out with someone, it might go against me.'

It was a lame excuse and it was obvious that Alex thought so, but he shrugged and said, 'All right, we won't let Jared know.'

She tried to put Alex off, really tried, but he was lonely, not having made many new friendships yet, and Purdey's life was empty anyway, so she found it hard to send him away. So they started going out together again, but Purdey refused to go to London with him; once had been enough. She had joined the local tennis club and Alex went along with her, driving over a couple of times a week. And they got into the habit of seeing each other at least once over the weekend, when Purdey didn't go home to see her mother and Toby. But quite often when she went there now she would find her mother's new friend, Derek Wilson, at the flat, and she often ended up baby-sitting while they went out. She had liked Derek from the start. He was a kind, patient man, and was obviously very fond of both her mother and Toby. And Toby and he got on like a house on fire. Whenever she went there Toby would proudly show off a new badge that he'd won at Scouts, and Derek was teaching him to swim too. 'And we're all going camping again,' Toby told Purdey, his eyes shining behind his glasses. 'Mum's coming too. Why don't you come with us?'

Purdey grinned, thinking that this was one holiday where her mother *wouldn't* want her to come along. 'I'd love to, Kiddo, but I have to work.'

Between work, seeing Alex, looking after the Gascoynes' house and occasional visits home, Purdey's life should have been pretty full, but it had never felt so empty. She didn't see Jared for several weeks, deliberately timing her trips to other hotels for Wednesdays, when the board meetings were held. But from what she gathered Jared had missed several of those too. She had picked a hotel some way away as the next one to be given leisure facilities, and spent quite a lot of time there with the architect and builders. And she went over to Jersey again several times, vainly trying to shut out all the memories the place brought back.

August came and, instead of summer weather, brought with it rain, and the only good news was that her mother and Derek Wilson were engaged and planned to be married quite soon. Purdey stood at her office window one afternoon looking out over the soaking gardens and hoping that the weather would clear before the weekend when her mother, Toby and Derek were due to go on their camping holiday. She could think of nothing worse than being in a tent in those conditions, and wondered whether they would cancel and go later.

The door opened behind her and Purdey turned with a smile that froze on her face as she saw that it was Jared. He glanced at her, looked away, and then back again.

'These letters about the Jersey hotel were addressed to me by mistake,' he told her, holding out some papers. 'I suppose because I went over there in the first place.'

'Thank you.' Purdey put down her coffee mug and took them from him. 'I'll—deal with them.'

'Good.' Jared shoved his hands in his pockets. 'Are you—all right?'

'Yes. Fine.' She looked at him in surprise at his sudden concern.

'I just wanted to be sure.'

She realised what he meant then and coloured

painfully. 'You don't have to worry,' she said shortly. 'There will be no aftermath.'

He nodded, seemed about to say something, but changed his mind and turned to go just as Simon walked in.

'Ah, there you are, Jared. I've been looking for you. The big boss wants a word with you in his office before you leave. Hello, Purdey.' Simon came over and planted a kiss on her cheek. 'How's things?'

'Great,' she answered over-brightly.

'Good.' He crossed to leave with Jared, but as they reached the door Simon turned and said casually, 'Give my regards to Alex next time you see him.'

'Yes, OK,' Purdey answered unheedingly, and then stood in horror as Jared's head turned round to stare at her. He gave her one killing glance and then strode out of the room with Simon following.

She half expected Jared to come back to her office later and have a go at her, but he didn't. But she knew he wouldn't leave it there. He had said there would be trouble if she saw Alex again, and he wasn't the kind of man who made idle threats. Admitting to herself that she was being a coward, Purdey left the office early that evening and drove home wondering what Jared would have done if she hadn't been OK, if there had been an aftermath to their night together in Jersey. Bitterly she decided that he was so used to using money to solve his problems that he would most likely have told her to have an abortion and he would pay—after checking to make sure she really was pregnant first of course. One thing was for sure; he would never have married her.

It was with these morose thoughts on her mind that

Purdey reached the cottage, and was surprised to see the Gascoynes' car outside the main house. She walked over, and Julia came to the door. 'Hello, Purdey, come on in.'

They sat down to chat in the kitchen over a cup of coffee, but Julia seemed rather ill at ease, seeming about to say something several times and then changing her mind.

In the end, Purdey said bluntly, 'Is anything the matter?'

Julia gave an embarrassed laugh. 'Yes, as a matter of fact, there is. We're going to sell the house. You see, Ned has been offered this absolutely super job in America, and naturally he wants to take us all with him. But I'm afraid we won't be able to keep this house on as well, much as we love it.'

'No, of course not,' Purdey agreed hollowly.

'It's rotten for you, I know, after we asked you to come and live here. I'm awfully sorry about that, Purdey.'

'Not at all. I've always been grateful that you asked me. When do you want me to move out?'

'Oh, not until the place is sold. And that could be months yet. But I thought I ought to tell you at once in case you wanted to make other arrangements.'

'I see. Well, thanks for letting me know.'

They talked a little longer, and then Julia left to drive back to London while Purdey went over to the cottage, thinking that this just wasn't her day. Kicking off her shoes, she fixed herself a long drink and then curled up in the armchair, thinking about Jared, letting the pain of seeing him again take over. She realised that if she had been pregnant she would never have told him, even though he'd asked. And she wouldn't have had an abortion, either. She would have loved his child as fiercely as she loved him.

Her thoughts occupied her for well over an hour, before someone beat a tattoo on the old iron knocker on her door, making her jump. She rose to open it and found Alex on her doorstep, dressed in a tracksuit and carrying his tennis gear.

'Oh, no,' Purdey groaned.

'That's a great welcome, I must say.' Alex's eyes went over her. 'You've forgotten our tennis date.'

'Yes, I'm afraid so.' She held the door for him to squeeze past her in the tiny hall. 'Sorry, but I've had things on my mind.'

'Problems at work?'

'No. The Gascoynes are selling up. I'll have to look for somewhere else to live.'

'That's a shame.' He went into the sitting-room and saw her empty glass. 'Been drowning your sorrows?'

'Mm. Would you like one?' She mixed him a drink, and when she gave it to him said, 'Would you mind if we didn't play tennis today, Alex? I really don't feel like it.'

'Of course not.' He sat down on the other side of the empty fireplace and said, 'Here, maybe this will cheer you up a little. I brought you an invitation to my birthday celebration.'

He passed her an envelope, and when Purdey opened it she found a printed invitation card to a dance to be held at a country mansion. She raised her eyebrows. 'It sounds very grand.'

Alex pulled a comical face. 'My mother insisted.'

'Does she know you've invited me?' Purdey asked

curiously.

'She doesn't know you.' Alex leaned forward earnestly. 'But I'd like her to. Purdey, will you come and meet my mother? Come and stay this weekend. There will be a few other people there. Please come, Purdey.'

She gave a definite shake of her head. 'It's kind of you, Alex, but I don't think so.'

'Why not?' Alex stepped across to her chair and went down on his knees beside her. 'Purdey, I want to hold you to your promise. I want you to marry me.'

'Alex, no.' She looked at him in distress. 'I told you right at the beginning that we could only be friends. Oh, I *knew* I should never have let you persuade me to go out with you again.'

'But we get on very well together, don't we?' Alex urged. 'And if we got married you wouldn't have to worry about finding somewhere to live—you wouldn't have to work at all.'

'Oh, Alex.' She shook her head at him and put out a hand to touch his hair. 'I'm very, very flattered, but I'm not the right girl for you. I never have been. I like you very much, I always have done. You're fun and you're nice. But you want a girl who will devote her whole time to you. I'm a career girl, Alex.'

'But surely you want to get married and have children?' he said in disbelief.

She shook her head. 'That's out of the question, I'm afraid.' Seeing the look of puzzled disappointment in his eyes, Purdey hesitated, then said, 'You were away a long time, Alex. Things—happened. I've changed, and so has my life. I can't marry you, I'm sorry.'

'You mean you're in love with someone else?'

Again she hesitated, but then nodded briefly.

'But you can't marry him?'

'No. There's no possibility of that.'

'He's already married, I suppose. Oh, Purdey, I'm sorry. I had no idea.' Putting his arms round her, Alex held her close, her head on his shoulder, giving her what comfort he could. And Purdey took it gratefully, her spirits at an all-time low.

'Such a touching scene!'

Jared's harsh voice made them turn in startled surprise to see him standing just inside the room, a look of cold determination on his grim face. 'The door was open, so I came in. Obviously you were too preoccupied to hear my knock,' he said sneeringly. Then added as Alex began to get to his feet, 'Oh, please don't let me disturb you. What were you doing—proposing?'

'Yes, as a matter of fact, I was,' Alex answered shortly. 'Not that it's anything to do with you, *Uncle*.' And he stressed the last word in a tone that made Purdey want to cheer.

'But I'm afraid it has a great deal to do with me, *nephew*,' Jared corrected him. 'I already warned you to stay away from her.'

'But you didn't give any reasons,' Alex pointed out. He drew himself up to his full height. 'And I'll decide for myself who I want to go out with—or marry, if it comes to that.'

'Then it seems that I shall have to enlighten you.' Jared turned to look down at Purdey where she sat in the chair. 'Unless of course you would like to tell Alex the edifying little tale yourself?' he suggested sarcastically.

'Oh, no, I wouldn't dream of spoiling your fun,' Purdey answered in a flat, withdrawn voice. 'And besides, I'm quite sure you'll do it so much better than I.'

Her tone brought a frown to Jared's brows, but Alex said, 'What is this? What are you getting at?' in indignant bewilderment and Jared turned to him.

'Four years ago your mother found out that you were getting serious about a gambling-club croupier.' He made a contemptuous gesture towards Purdey. 'She asked me to intervene. So I did.'

'Intervene? How? I don't understand.'

'It's quite simple, Alex. I offered Purdey a sum of money to keep away from you, and she took it—after some haggling. I bought her off,' he said bluntly.

'Bought her off?' Alex's face had gone very white. 'You mean that's—that's why she went away?'

'Yes. That was part of the bargain.'

Alex stared at him, not wanting to believe it. Then he swung round to Purdey. 'Is this true?'

She nodded. 'Yes, Alex. I'm sorry.'

'And I suppose that was why I was sent away to Canada. Damn you, Jared. Damn you both!' He took a hasty step towards Purdey and pulled her to her feet. 'Didn't you feel anything for me, anything at all?'

'She set you up,' Jared said harshly from behind him. 'She told me herself that she had no intention of marrying you—but not until after she'd got the money, of course. And she admitted that she wasn't in love with you; she told me *that* the first time she went to bed with *me*.'

Alex turned on Purdey, his face dreadful, then raised his hand and would have hit her if Jared hadn't caught his arm. 'Hold hard, old son, she isn't worth it.'

'Damn you, let go of me!' Alex pushed Jared aside and strode out of the room, and a minute later they heard his car driving away.

Purdey sighed and put a tired hand up to her brow before going over to pour herself a drink.

'It seems I've spoiled your little game yet again,' Jared remarked caustically.

'And lost your nephew's respect in the bargain.'

'You're taking it very coolly, considering you've lost a fortune.'

'Have I?'

'Alex is a very rich young man. Think of all the money you would have had to squander if you'd succeeded in marrying him,' he pointed out jeeringly.

She turned to him with a shrug. 'I'll survive.'

He frowned. 'Don't tell me you're a good loser.'

'I'm not telling you anything.'

Jared's face hardened and he stepped towards her. 'There's still one matter we have to settle, you and I.' He put his hand under her chin, tilting her head so that she had to look at him. 'You didn't keep your part of the bargain. I warned Alex to keep away from you and I thought he had, but you persuaded him to see you behind my back, encouraging him to fall for you again.' His mouth twisted. 'You need to be punished for that.'

Purdey gave a harsh laugh and moved away from him. 'I thought I already had been.'

'My telling Alex the truth was hardly a punishment.'

'I didn't mean now, I meant—in Jersey.' And, try

as she might, Purdey was unable to keep a catch out of her voice.

'That wasn't a punishment.' He came to stand behind her. 'Not for you. Although you tried to use it as one on me.'

Slowly Purdey turned to face him, her eyes wide in her set face. 'Is that what you think?'

He gave a thin smile. 'Do you think I don't know women? By acting the victim, you were trying to make me feel guilty.'

'And did you?'

His smile deepened, because sinister. 'What if I told you there was a way you could recoup some of the money you lost by not marrying Alex?'

She looked at him in perplexity, thrown by his abrupt change of mood. 'I don't follow.'

'It's quite simple. How would you like to make—say ten thousand pounds? And have all your expenses paid for a year?'

Her eyes widened. 'And what would I have to do for all this largesse?'

Jared put his hands on her shoulders. 'I think you already know that.'

She caught her breath. 'But I'd like you to spell it out to me.'

'All right. I'd want you to become my mistress. And to make me—happy.'

Her face tightened. 'And to do that I suppose I would have to—to respond to your—lovemaking?'

'Of course.'

'Even if I didn't feel like it?'

'You do—only you won't let yourself.'

Purdey stepped back and turned away from him,

filled with the coldest anger that she had ever known. 'And you think that money will—will lower my defences, do you?'

'I'm sure of it—given enough.'

Swinging round, Purdey looked into his mocking face. 'But you haven't offered enough.'

'No? Then just how much do you want for the exclusive rights to your body?' Jared demanded roughly.

'You'll just have to make me an offer I can't refuse, won't you? After all, everyone has their price. Isn't that the maxim you live by? But I warn you, mine is very high.'

He came to loom over her, anger in his face now as he heard the scorn in her voice. 'So what is the price—another thirty-five thousand? But would you be worth it? I wonder.'

'You should know,' Purdey reminded him acidly. 'You already sampled what I have to offer. Think of what was—and what could be. Especially if I did what you wanted. Like this.' And, stepping forward, Purdey put her arms round his neck, her hand in his hair, and slowly drew his head down to kiss him. She put everything she had into that kiss, and soon his arms went round her and held her close against him. But all the time she kissed him in such sexual passion, the cold rage was growing, taking over her heart and mind.

Eventually he let her go, and Purdey stepped back as they stared at each other. 'All right,' Jared growled thickly at last, 'you'll get your thirty-five thousand pounds.'

Purdey looked at him in cool mockery, enjoying the

power she had over him. 'But I don't remember mentioning that figure.'

His eyes narrowed. 'What, then? But I warn you not to try me too far, or you'll lose out.'

'Will I?' She lifted her head and pretended to look at him consideringly, but her mind working fast, searching for a price he wouldn't be able to pay. 'I lost a great deal by not marrying Alex, and I think it only right that you should make it up to me.'

'Damn you, Purdey. What do you want?'

'Why, the one thing that can ever repay me. I want—marriage.'

Jared stared at her, for a moment frozen into immobility, then he said curtly, 'You just priced yourself out of the market.'

Purdey's lips curled. 'If you can't stand the heat, get out of the kitchen.' Her temper suddenly flaring, she yelled, 'And get out of my life. Go on. Get out. I never want to see you again.'

She made as if to push him, but Jared caught her flailing arm. 'Why, you little . . .'

His words were cut off as Purdey picked up her glass with her free hand and threw the contents in his face. 'You swine!' she shouted. 'I wouldn't want you at any price.'

Within any relationship between a man and a woman there was a fundamental antagonism, a primitive savagery that was always waiting to break out once the barriers went down. Purdey had gone crashing through those barriers and was suddenly terrified by the consequences. Jared's eyes darkened with rage. He tore the glass from her hand and threw it into the fireplace, so violently that it shattered into minute pieces. Then he put her hands behind her back and jerked her towards him.

Purdey had never been so afraid in her life, but within that fear was a crazy kind of exultation because she had the power to arouse so much emotion in him. Maybe some inner part of her had wanted this all along, making her deliberately provoke his fury.

But, lifting her head, Purdey said fiercely, 'If you touch me, I'll tell the police.'

'Will you?' Jared glared at her almost unheedingly, too angry to care. 'Everything becomes physical with you. It always has. Love, hate . . .' Then he put his free hand behind her head and kissed her.

It took Purdey long, reluctant moments to surface from that kiss. It was like coming awake from a wonderful dream. Slowly she opened her eyes to stare at Jared, her breath suspended, her body weak and heavy with desire.

His eyes glinted down at her, still angry, but there was passion there too now. 'Will you?' he repeated.

Dimly, she remembered her threat and shook her head. 'No,' she breathed.

'I thought not,' he said, and picked her up to carry her into the bedroom.

CHAPTER EIGHT

THERE was very little traffic on the roads as Purdey drove from the cottage up to London, and it was still only seven in the morning when she drew up outside her mother's flat. Just a little over two hours since she'd woken and found that Jared had gone. History repeating itself, she thought in painful bitterness. It was too early to go and knock on the door, so Purdey sat in the car and watched the street gradually come to life, with nightworkers returning home, grey and tired; the paper-boy whistling as he shoved the papers through letter flaps; and the milkman with his electric trolley, clattering along. The sun came out, low in the sky, shining through the windscreen into her eyes. And it was this that made them prick with tears, not the fact that she felt so bereft and used.

At eight Purdey took one of her hastily packed suitcases from the car and went up the steps to the main door of the house and rang her mother's bell. Toby came down to let her in, exclaiming with surprise when he saw her. He was too old for hugs and kisses now, but he gave her a big grin and manfully offered to carry her case.

'Why, thanks.' Purdey gave him her car keys. 'And you'll find the rest of my stuff in the car.'

His eyebrows rose. 'You want me to bring all of it in?'

'Just the suitcases for now.'

She went up the stairs to the flat and found her mother in the kitchen, making breakfast. Mrs Bruce turned round to her with a surprised smi e, but then saw her daughter's face and said, 'Oh, Purdey, love.' And put her arms around her.

Purdey promptly burst into tears and clung to her mother for several minutes before she could even begin to try and control herself. Then she started to say broken words all mixed up with apologies, but was still shaken by sobs so that the words didn't make any sense.

'Here, sit down. Drink this.' Helen Bruce pushed her gently into a chair and put a cup of strong coffee into Purdey's hands. 'Now, darling, try and tell me what's the matter.' And she gently stroked the hair back from her desolate face.

'I—I can't.' Purdey gripped the cup tightly as fresh tears spilled down her cheeks.

'Is it a man?'

Purdey gulped, then closed her eyes painfully and nodded. 'Oh, Mum, I love him so much.'

'Drink your coffee, love, it will make you feel better,' her mother said helplessly. 'Then just tell me as much as you want to.'

'You'll be late for work,' Purdey protested weakly.

'That doesn't matter. I'll phone and tell them. Oh, here's Toby, he can do it.'

Her brother stopped short when he saw Purdey crying, then came up and put an awkward hand on her shoulder, fear and worry in his eyes. 'Is Purdey ill?' His biggest terror since his own illness had been that someone he loved would become ill too.

'No,' their mother reassured him and sent him to phone and then go to school. Then she sat with Purdey and gradually got most of the story out of her, finding out for the first time where the money for Toby's operation had come from. 'I've always been afraid of something like this,' she sighed. 'But I didn't dare to ask at the time; we needed the money so desperately.'

'I've been saving up to pay it back,' Purdey said dully, 'but I don't have enough yet.'

'So have I,' Mrs Bruce admitted. 'I didn't believe what you said about a philanthropist, although I tried to at the time, but I haven't saved very much I'm afraid. Only just over three thousand pounds.'

'Oh, Mum, you ought to spend that on your wedding,' Purdey said in distress.

'Debts come first,' her mother insisted. 'And besides, Derek and I don't want a fancy wedding. Just a simple ceremony with you and Toby as witnesses will make us very happy. And you must come and live here for as long as you like. As a matter of fact, I was going to ask you to come and look after Toby while we're on our honeymoon. Will you do that for me?'

'Yes, of course. You know I will.'

'What about your job?'

Purdey shook her head. 'I'm not going back, I might see—see Jared again there. I'll write to them today and let them know. And I must return the car somehow, too.'

'We'll work out a way. I can always borrow Derek's car and follow you down there and bring you back.'

And that was what they did that evening, when Purdey was sure that the offices would be empty, afterwards sealing the car keys into an envelope with her letter of resignation and pushing it through the letterbox. The envelope fell into the basket on the other side, ending the best job she'd ever had, ending her career for good probably, because she would never be able to ask the group for a reference, and who could get a decent job nowadays without a reference?

The next day, though, Purdey did get a job, one that she walked into off the street and was far below her capabilities. A mindless job that ordinarily would have driven her mad with boredom, but which suited her now as she tried to think what she was going to do in the future. Remembering how she'd felt after Jersey, she realised that the same things still applied; it would be best for her to go right away, even leave the country. But first she had the eternal problem of paying Jared back, and even with the money her mother had saved they were still nearly fifteen thousand pounds short.

Purdey tried hard not to think of Jared, but it was impossible not to. Her life had changed from the moment he entered it, and always for the worse, it seemed. And yet she knew now that she had been in love with him since the first time that he had kissed her, so long ago. Why else would other men's kisses have meant nothing to her? She thought of that night in Jersey and wished that she hadn't been so stubborn, and so full of angry pride. If she'd given herself to him fully, then things might have been so different. At least the memories would have been kinder. And all she had now was memories. But she couldn't bring herself to remember that last night together. That was still too painful, still too raw and hurting.

The future seemed bleak whichever way she looked at it, and even Purdey's natural optimism couldn't rise above the desolation in her heart. She would have to find somewhere to live soon, she realised, because she wouldn't want to live at the flat when her mother and Derek got back from their honeymoon, but somehow she couldn't summon up the energy to even start.

She had been home for nearly two weeks when her mother waited until Toby had gone to bed one evening and then said, 'I have something for you.'

Purdey glanced up from the magazine she was merely gazing at and saw the gleam of excitement in her mother's eyes. 'What is it?'

'Here, take a look.' And Helen Bruce handed Purdey a cheque for fifteen thousand pounds!

Her mouth fell open as Purdey stared at it in stunned disbelief. Then she found her voice. 'But—but this is from Derek's account.'

'I know, but he wants you to take it to pay off our debt.'

'You told him?'

'Yes. Don't look so worried, I only told him that we still owed the money. Nothing about you and this man. So Derek went out and borrowed the money against some property his mother left him.'

'But I can't take Derek's money,' Purdey exclaimed in horror, and pushed the cheque back.

'He's not giving it to you,' her mother rejoined. 'He's giving it to Toby. He loves Toby very much, you know.' She smiled. 'Sometimes I wonder who's the main attraction, Toby or me. He said if he'd known us then he would have raised all the money for Toby's operation. In fact, he wanted to give me more, but I would only take what we needed. Most of the rest I owe to you.'

'Oh, Mum, don't be silly.'

'It isn't right that you've had to carry this burden by yourself all these years.'

Purdey smiled. 'I can take it.' Her face shadowed. 'Or I could once.'

'Well, now you'll be able to give the money back, won't you? You'll have that off your mind at least.'

Purdey nodded and stood up. 'I must go round and thank Derek straight away.'

Her mother grinned. 'He'll like that.' And then gasped as Purdey gave her a tremendous hug.

The next day Purdey purchased an anonymous money order for the whole amount and sent it to Jared care of his bank in an envelope marked 'Personal' and for his attention. Perhaps he would guess who it came from, but he would never know how she had raised the money. Although he would very likely think the worst, she realised bitterly. But at least she was free of this great weight on her shoulders at last. She even felt physically lighter, although that was probably because she hadn't felt like eating much lately.

The wedding was a week later, in their local church in its oasis of green among the city streets. It was a very simple service, but very moving, with just a few friends and relatives there. But when they came out of the church there were all the Scouts in Derek's troop lined up to form a guard of honour, and a photographer friend to take photographs of them all. Afterwards there was a wedding breakfast at which Toby ate far more than anyone else, and then the bride and groom left for their honeymoon in Spain.

Purdey and Toby were left to take the wedding presents back to the flat and talk over the day until Toby's head began to droop and he agreed with Purdey that it was time for bed.

When he'd gone, Purdey sat in a chair with just a lamp to light the room, her thoughts wistful, and even though she tried to concentrate on other things her mind kept drifting back to Jared, and in the end she surrendered and let herself think of that last night together at last.

It had started off in such anger on Jared's side; he had been furious about Alex, and even more furious of her rejection of his offer. He had expected the same passive resistance that she'd shown in Jersey and at first she had hung back a little, but her own anger had soon been submerged by the aching need to hold him and to give this time as well as take. And that night she had murmured his name and whispered words of love and need while he had made love to her, had responded as avidly as the most ardent lover could desire.

And gradually she had felt his anger recede as Jared grew more passionate, his own hunger fuelled by her unexpected reaction. They had shared love then, glorying in the delight they aroused in one another, filled with the wonder and beauty of the other's body, and lifting each other to shared heights of sensual excitement. And it seemed so long that they had been apart that soon Jared was raining kisses on her again, his body already aroused and hungry.

Afterwards, as they lay spent and exhausted, Purdey had turned within his arms and buried her head against his neck. 'I love you,' she murmured, her lips on his skin. 'I love you so much.' She didn't know whether he heard, she didn't think he had, but it didn't matter, she had said what was in her heart.

He had made love to her once more, slowly and gently at first, making her moan and cry out in delight, but as she arched her quivering body towards him he had suddenly changed and taken her in primitive savagery that made him groan and groan again in an agony of pleasure until he had dropped exhausted by her side.

They had slept then, Purdey in the deep, peaceful sleep that only sexual happiness brings, and she hadn't woken until some slight noise had roused her, and she had reached out and found that Jared had gone. Left her like a man leaving a one-night stand that he would never see again.

Now tears gathered in Purdey's eyes, but she found that she was fiercely glad that she'd responded and shown him how she really felt. That night had been open and wonderful, and she would have it to remember for the rest of her life. Getting to her feet, Purdey switched off the lamp and went to bed, empty and alone.

September was as sunny as August had been wet. The bride and groom rang from Spain to say they were having a wonderful time and asked anxiously how she was. Purdey reassured her mother as best she could, but didn't deceive her for a minute. She kept on with her boring job because she just didn't feel like finding anything better, but she did rouse herself to try and find somewhere to live, a task that was as depressing as it was useless.

Purdey usually went to look at places in her lunch

break or on the way home from work. Toby finished school and was always home before her; he had his own key, so she had no need to worry about him. She went to see one abysmally damp and dirty place one afternoon, and couldn't get back to the flat quickly enough. At least it was dry and clean, even if it was small. As she opened the front door Purdey heard Toby's voice and guessed he'd brought a friend home, which he often did. A popular boy was Toby. She hung up her jacket and noticed her windswept hair in the mirror, but couldn't be bothered to go and brush it.

'Hello, kiddo. Had a good day? I didn't . . .' Purdey came to an abrupt stop as the man Toby was talking to rose to his feet and turned towards her. 'J-Jared!'

'Hello, Purdey.'

'He said he was a friend of yours, so I let him in. Was that all right?' Toby asked looking anxiously at her stunned face.

'What? Oh, yes, I—I suppose so.' She gazed at Jared, her heart doing crazy somersaults. 'What—what do you want?' she asked painfully.

'To talk to you.' His eyes were fixed on her face, his features tense. 'To ask you to . . .'

But Purdey gave an abrupt shake of her head. 'I have nothing to say to you.'

'But I have a great many things I want to say to you,' Jared told her tersely.

He took a step towards her, but Purdey instinctively backed away. Toby, who had been looking from one to the other of them, stepped in front of Purdey and looked up at Jared belligerently, his hands balling into fists. 'Are you the one who made my sister cry?' he demanded.

Jared looked down at him for a moment and then at Purdey, and said gravely, 'Yes, I'm rather afraid I am. That's why I've come here,' he added. 'To ask her to forgive me.'

Purdey could find nothing to say to that and she looked away, but her eyes fell on a photograph album that lay open on the coffee-table and she grew suddenly still.

'Yes,' Jared said, following her gaze, 'Toby has been telling me all about his trips to America and the operations he had on his eyes *four years ago.*'

Reaching out, Purdey put her hands on Toby's shoulders and said, 'Toby, why don't you go and do your homework?'

He turned to face her. 'You want me out of the way, I suppose?'

'Yes, please.'

'Well, all right, only—I'm hungry. Shall I go in the kitchen and start making dinner instead?'

'How about a takeaway?' Jared suggested. 'Is there one nearby?'

'There's a Kentucky Fried Chicken and a McDonalds,' Toby told him hopefully.

'Why don't you get whatever you think best?' And Jared took a note from his pocket and gave it to him.

Toby looked at it and gave it back. 'That's far too much.'

Jared was about to say something, but looked into Toby's open young face, and took the note back to replace it with a lesser one. 'Get enough for the three of us,' he told him. 'Oh, and Toby—take your time. OK?'

Toby reached the door, looked back and grinned. 'OK.'

When he'd gone Purdey said tartly, 'Resorting to the bribery and corruption of infants now? How very like you. I'm surprised you didn't tell him to keep the change.'

His jaw hardened a little but Jared said lightly, 'When a man's desperate, he resorts to desperate measures.'

She gave a thin laugh. 'You? Desperate? I don't believe it's possible.'

'Well, that's where you're wrong. Because I've been desperately trying to find you.'

Not knowing how to take that, Purdey looked at him searchingly for a moment and then quickly away. 'How—how did you find me?'

'By detective work. By using the Inland Revenue and the Health Insurance people, by going through your file and contacting your old employers, talking to the people you used to work with. That narrowed it down to London, and this . . .' He paused, taking an envelope from his pocket. 'This envelope had a postmark, and this money order inside it had a bank stamp which led to this area. Then it was simply a matter of going through the electoral rolls and eliminating all the other people named Bruce until I found you.'

As he spoke, he took the money order out of the envelope and held it up. 'Why did you send me this?'

'I?' She pretended to read it and then shrugged. 'I don't know what you're talking about. It has nothing to do with me.'

'Damn you, don't lie to me.' Jared's voice was

suddenly sharp and angry. 'I *know* you sent it.'

Purdey's chin came up defiantly. 'You're mistaken.'

'Am I?' He looked at her. 'Well, it's obviously been sent to the wrong person, then.' And he began to tear the order into pieces.

With a gasp of horror, Purdey ran to stop him. 'No, you can't! If you only knew how long it took to save . . .' She stopped abruptly and drew back, biting her lip.

Throwing the torn scraps aside, Jared caught her wrist. 'Why didn't you tell me what you wanted the money for?' he demanded harshly.

'I couldn't. It was *my* problem. How could I possibly tell you? And anyway, you'd only have thought it a sob story that I'd made up.'

Jared's grip tightened. 'Maybe I would, at that,' he admitted. 'But you could have told me since then. You could easily have told me when we were in Jersey.'

'What difference would it have made? You still wouldn't have believed me. You were always ready to believe the worst of me, right from the first. That's why I took the money from you; because you were so damn superior and insulting.' She stopped, her breathing unsteady, and snatched her wrist away from him so that she could move away from his over-powering presence. After a moment she said bitterly, 'As a matter of fact, I was about to tell you once. But Alex came along and you, of course, immediately put the worst interpretation you could on it.'

His face grim, Jared said, 'I talked to Alex when I was trying to find you; he told me that you turned him down. You said that you *couldn't* marry him. Was that because of me? *Are* you in love with him?'

'Aren't you a bit late asking that question?' Purdey said acidly. 'You never bothered to ask it when you tried to buy me off him, so why ask it now?'

Jared took an angry stride towards her. *'Because I have to damn well know.'*

Her voice tight in her throat, Purdey looked up into his taut face and said, 'No, I—I'm not in love with Alex.'

His features relaxed a fraction, but Jared's voice was still fierce as he said, 'Then that leaves the next question: why did you take off from the cottage that night?'

Purdey's eyes widened as she stared at him. 'Why did *I* take off? Because you'd already left, of course; walked away as if I was some common tramp you'd just picked up. I . . .' She stopped as realisation came and raised stunned eyes to meet his. 'You mean you went back?'

'Yes, I went back,' Jared said heavily. 'I woke up in the night and realised that I had a hell of a lot of thinking to do. So I dressed and went out into the garden.' His mouth twisted wryly. 'I was trying to reconcile what I knew about you with how I felt about you. I must have walked around for some time, I don't know how long, and then I heard a car driving away. When I reached the cottage, I found it locked and your car gone.'

'Oh.' Purdey's legs felt suddenly weak and she leaned back against the wall.

Jared looked at her broodingly. 'I did think you were a tramp at first,' he admitted. 'But I didn't think you were a danger because I was sure Alex would get over you, but then I saw you with him at the rugby match, without make-up and looking so lovely, so different. I thought that if you could make such an impression on me, then you would easily lure Alex, who was so much younger and more impressionable, into marriage.' He paused before saying tightly, 'And I didn't want you to marry Alex—even then. I think that was why I was willing to pay any price you asked to make you leave.'

Purdey had become very still as she listened to him, and found no words to say. Jared thrust his hands in his pockets and turned to walk a few paces away from her, but swung round as he said fiercely, 'When I saw you again I was glad, I told myself I'd be able to pay you back, especially after I saw you with Simon. But when there was an excuse not to get rid of you, I took it. And I deliberately promoted your ideas for the Jersey hotel and arranged it so that I went over with you. Because I was attracted to you, had been all along.' His voice grew suddenly bleak. 'Fatally attracted. I went to Jersey with the express intention of going to bed with you, although I wouldn't admit it to myself. But when I did—and found you so innocent, and so defiant . . .'

He broke off as words failed him, and took several more agitated paces before he went on, 'I didn't know what to think. One moment I hated myself for what I'd done, and the next I'd remember that you were a cold-blooded little cheat. Then I hoped that maybe you had a reason and I could get you to tell me. But as you said, Alex came along and I jumped to the obvious conclusion. I tried to warn him off you without telling him why, and I thought I'd succeeded.

But then Simon let slip that you were still seeing him, and I found you together at the cottage.' His face grew white with remembered rage. 'I don't think I've ever been so angry in all my life as I was then. I was determined that he wouldn't have you. And I didn't care what I said or did to break you up.'

'But you couldn't leave it there,' Purdey said into the taut silence. 'You couldn't just walk away. You had to—punish me first. Isn't that what you said?'

Stepping forward, Jared put a hand on her arm, his body shaking with tension. 'It may have been what I said, but all I wanted was to make love to you again. I was angry, yes, damn angry. I thought that all the worst things I'd ever believed about you were true. I thought that there was no hope for us. I was sure that you would defy me again and that would keep my anger alive. But then . . .' His voice faltered painfully. 'But then you were so loving, so passionate in return. You said—I almost believed that you said you loved me.' On that, his eyes searched her face, but Purdey hastily looked down. 'I wasn't sure. I had to think. So when I woke I went out for that walk in the garden.'

'I—I see,' Purdey faltered after a long moment.

'Do you?' Jared's lips twisted in self-mockery. 'Don't you want to know what conclusion I reached that night? Or why I've been searching for you?'

Filled with a sudden panic, Purdey pushed herself away from him. 'No! No, I don't want to know. If you've said all you came to say, then I wish you'd go away.'

'But I haven't said all that I came to say. There's one thing left.' His voice had changed, become soft, and Purdey turned away, her heart so large in her chest she could hardly breathe. 'Tell me, Purdey, why have you never married?' he asked unexpectedly.

'Married?' She turned to him with a gasp of laughter. 'You must be joking!'

'Why? Because you've never met anyone?'

'Mind your own damn business,' she retorted.

'But I want to make it my business. So tell me, why is the idea of marriage such a joke?'

'Why is it a joke? How the hell did you expect me to marry someone and then confess to my husband that I owed another man thirty-five thousand pounds?'

For a moment Jared looked taken aback, but then he said insistently, 'But that wasn't the only reason, was it? Do you remember the first time I kissed you?' Purdey's eyes leapt to his face and he gave a small nod of satisfaction. 'I thought you did. I couldn't get that out of my mind. I couldn't get you out of my mind. And through all those years I felt as if I was waiting for something. But it took me a while to realise I was waiting for you. And I'm hoping against hope that it was the same for you. I love you, Purdey. I want you to marry me. That's what I came back to tell you at the cottage that night.'

Purdey stared at him for a long moment, bereft of speech, but then she gave a long sigh. 'So, just like that,' she said unsteadily, 'you find out that I wanted the money for a good cause and everything's all right, is it?'

'I realised I was in love with you *before* I found out about the money,' Jared corrected her.

'So you did.' But Purdey's face didn't soften. 'Ever since I met you again you've made my life hell,' she said fiercely. 'And now you walk in here and expect me to marry you, not just forgive you. Why the hell should I?'

'Purdey, I know and I'm sorry. But please try to see it from my point of view; everything was against you —everything but this terrible longing I had to be with you, to love you.'

'But you turned even that against me, didn't you? And when did you ever try to see it from my point of view?' she pointed out tartly. 'The answer's no, I won't marry you.'

His face very pale, Jared stepped towards her. 'You can't mean that.' He went to take her in his arms, but saw the flash of anger in her eyes. 'I *know* you're in love with me,' he said forcefully. 'That night we spent together at the cottage proved that.'

'Maybe it did,' Purdey admitted, but held up her hand as he moved towards her. 'But you asked me to marry you and the answer is still no.'

Jared drew back, his eyes bleak, but then he said grimly, 'I see. I'm to be punished, am I?' He turned away but then said tightly, 'Do you know what I've been through these last few weeks, not knowing where you were, petrified that I'd lost you and would never see you again?'

'Yes,' Purdey answered unsteadily. 'I know *exactly* what it was like.'

He swung towards her. 'Then surely . . .'

But she shook her head firmly. 'Goodbye, Jared.' And, going over to the door, she opened it for him to leave.

He stared at her, unable to accept that she meant it. 'I don't give up that easily,' he warned her. 'I'll come back.'

'And if you do the answer will still be the same. Will you please go now?'

He moved slowly to the door, his eyes fixed on her face, unable to accept defeat and filled with a terrible urge to just sweep her into his arms and *make* her say yes. But the firmness and determination in Purdey's face held him back, and after a few moments he turned on his heel and strode away.

Purdey closed the door after him and almost fell into a chair, all the indignation and resolve that had sustained her draining away and leaving her feeling weak both physically and mentally. She sat in the chair for a long time, thinking over what Jared had said, giving it time to warm her heart, time to decide what she was going to do. When Toby came home she was still sitting there, but jumped up to take the large bag he was carrying from him. 'Good heavens, what a lot!'

'I thought Mr Faulkner might be hungry. Where is he?' he asked, looking round.

'He had to leave. Good grief, we'll be eating chicken for a week. Never mind.' She smiled at Toby and pointed to the torn money order. 'And after we've eaten I've got a job for you. See all those scraps of paper on the floor? I want you to piece them together again.'

The next couple of days were very busy ones. Ignoring Jared's phone calls and the flowers he sent her, Purdey quit her job, spent an embarrassing half-hour at the bank explaining about the maltreated money order and getting her money back, and then went up to the West End and spent what was for her a huge amount on a designer evening dress, and the most beautiful, gossamer silk underwear. She hired a chauffeur-driven car and arranged for Toby to spend the weekend at a friend's house. On the Saturday afternoon she had her hair done at one of the best stylists in town, and in the evening put on all her new clothes.

When she was ready Purdey looked at her reflection in the full-length mirror in her mother's room and was satisfied that she was looking at her best. Her hair was swept off her face but fell loose at the back, and her dress, a slim gold sheath with huge but short puff sleeves, was both fashionable and becoming. She looked good and she knew it, happily blowing a kiss to her reflection before turning to leave.

Alex's birthday party was well under way when her car drew up outside the house he'd inherited from his grandfather. A doorman came to help her out of the car and usher her inside, where she handed her invitation to the man whose duty it was to keep out gatecrashers. The arriving guests were thinning out now, but Alex and his mother were still standing at the entrance to the ballroom.

When Alex saw her his head came up and his cheeks flushed a little, but he stepped forward to meet her and took her hand. 'Hello, Purdey.'

'Hello, Alex. Happy birthday.'

'You look—absolutely stunning.'

She smiled. 'Thank you.'

'Jared, he—er—explained about that money. I'm sorry if I—I offended you.'

'It doesn't matter, Alex. You had every right to be angry.'

Impulsively he leant forward to kiss her on the

cheek, then tucked her arm through his. 'Come and
meet my mother and then dance with me, will you?'

'Of course.'

'Mother, I'd like you to meet a very special lady.'
Lady Nash had been watching them with interest, but
a look of shock came into her eyes when she heard
Purdey's name and realised that this was the girl her
son had been sent abroad to forget. But she was given
no time to comment as Alex whisked Purdey away
and began to waltz her round the room.

'You've no need to search around,' Alex told her in
some amusement a few minutes later. 'He's here.'

Purdey looked at him and laughed happily, and a
few moments later had the satisfaction of seeing Jared
come to a dead stop in the middle of the floor as he
caught sight of her. He said some word to his partner
and then abandoned the poor woman to her fate as he
strode purposefully through the throng and came up
to them.

'This is my dance, I think,' he said grimly.

Alex looked at Purdey. 'What do you think, shall we
take pity on him?'

'Well, I don't know.' Purdey pretended to consider
it, but Jared firmly pushed Alex out of the way and
drew her into his arms.

'You minx, I ought to put you over my knee,' he
told her, his voice rough and unsteady. 'Why
wouldn't you answer my phone calls?'

'You know why.'

He sighed and relaxed a little, but held her close in
his strong arms, almost as if he was afraid of losing
her again. 'Well, at least you're here. And you look
enchanting, my love. My dearest love.'

'But not your *only* love,' she mocked.

The music paused between numbers and Jared looked down at her, his face sharpened by urgency and tension. 'You're the only woman I'll ever love,' he swore fervently. A flush of colour heightened Purdey's cheeks, and he said desperately, 'Look, let's go somewhere we can be alone, where we can talk this thing through.'

She shook her head. 'No, because I only have one thing to say to you.'

Jared stiffened, his face growing bleak and shook his head. 'No. Not yet. I . . .'

'And that,' Purdey continued relentlessly, 'is to tell you that I love you very much, my darling. So, will *you* marry *me*?'

He stared at her for a moment, his eyes widening, then gave a great shout of happiness that made everyone in the room turn to look. He lifted her off her feet and swung her round, before taking her in his arms to kiss her long and lingeringly.

The music had started again and couples were dancing round, smiling with amusement as they passed, before he let her go.

Purdey emerged, flushed and breathless and stammered, 'Hey, you—you didn't answer the question.'

Jared smiled down at her, his face alive with happiness. 'Yes,' he said simply. 'Yes, now and forever.' And he drew her into his arms to dance on into the future together.

HARLEQUIN
American Romance®

November brings you...

SENTIMENTAL JOURNEY

BARBARA BRETTON

Jitterbugging at the Stage Door Canteen, singing along with the Andrews Sisters, planting your Victory Garden—this was life on the home front during World War II.

Barbara Bretton captures all the glorious memories of America in the 1940's in SENTIMENTAL JOURNEY—a nostalgic Century of American Romance book and a Harlequin Award of Excellence title.

Available wherever Harlequin® books are sold.

ARSENT-1

You'll flip . . . your pages won't!
Read paperbacks *hands-free* with

Book Mate · I

The perfect "mate" for all your romance paperbacks

Traveling • Vacationing • At Work • In Bed • Studying • Cooking • Eating

Perfect size for all standard paperbacks, this wonderful invention makes reading a pure pleasure! Ingenious design holds paperback books OPEN and FLAT so even wind can't ruffle pages — leaves your hands free to do other things. Reinforced, wipe-clean vinyl-covered holder flexes to let you turn pages without undoing the strap . . . supports paperbacks so well, they have the strength of hardcovers!

Pages turn WITHOUT opening the strap

SEE-THROUGH STRAP

Reinforced back stays flat

Built in bookmark

BOOK MARK

BACK COVER HOLDING STRIP

10 x 7¼ opened
Snaps closed for easy carrying, too

Available now. Send your name, address, and zip code, along with a check or money order for just $5.95 + .75¢ for delivery (for a total of $6.70) payable to Reader Service to:

Reader Service
Bookmate Offer
3010 Walden Avenue
P.O. Box 1396
Buffalo, N.Y. 14269-1396

Offer not available in Canada
*New York residents add appropriate sales tax.

BM-GR

PASSPORT TO ROMANCE VACATION SWEEPSTAKES

OFFICIAL RULES

SWEEPSTAKES RULES AND REGULATIONS. NO PURCHASE NECESSARY.

HOW TO ENTER:

1. To enter, complete this official entry form and return with your invoice in the envelope provided, or print your name, address, telephone number and age on a plain piece of paper and mail to: Passport to Romance, P.O. Box #1397, Buffalo, N.Y. 14269-1397 No mechanically reproduced entries accepted.

2. All entries must be received by the Contest Closing Date, midnight, December 31, 1990 to be eligible.

3. Prizes: There will be ten (10) Grand Prizes awarded, each consisting of a choice of a trip for two people to: i) London, England (approximate retail value $5,050 U.S.); ii) England, Wales and Scotland (approximate retail value $6,400 U.S.); iii) Caribbean Cruise (approximate retail value $7,300 U.S.); iv) Hawaii (approximate retail value $ 9,550 U.S.); v) Greek Island Cruise in the Mediterranean (approximate retail value $12,250 U.S.); vi) France (approximate retail value $7,300 U.S.).

4. Any winner may choose to receive any trip or a cash alternative prize of $5,000.00 U.S. in lieu of the trip.

5. Odds of winning depend on number of entries received.

6. A random draw will be made by Nielsen Promotion Services, an independent judging organization on January 29, 1991, in Buffalo, N.Y., at 11:30 a.m. from all eligible entries received on or before the Contest Closing Date. Any Canadian entrants who are selected must correctly answer a time-limited, mathematical skill-testing question in order to win. Quebec residents may submit any litigation respecting the conduct and awarding of a prize in this contest to the Régie des loteries et courses du Quebec.

7. Full contest rules may be obtained by sending a stamped, self-addressed envelope to: "Passport to Romance Rules Request", P.O. Box 9998, Saint John, New Brunswick, E2L 4N4.

8. Payment of taxes other than air and hotel taxes is the sole responsibility of the winner.

9. Void where prohibited by law.

PASSPORT TO ROMANCE VACATION SWEEPSTAKES

OFFICIAL RULES

SWEEPSTAKES RULES AND REGULATIONS. NO PURCHASE NECESSARY.

HOW TO ENTER:

1. To enter, complete this official entry form and return with your invoice in the envelope provided, or print your name, address, telephone number and age on a plain piece of paper and mail to: Passport to Romance, P.O. Box #1397, Buffalo, N.Y. 14269-1397 No mechanically reproduced entries accepted.

2. All entries must be received by the Contest Closing Date, midnight, December 31, 1990 to be eligible.

3. Prizes: There will be ten (10) Grand Prizes awarded, each consisting of a choice of a trip for two people to: i) London, England (approximate retail value $5,050 U.S.); ii) England, Wales and Scotland (approximate retail value $6,400 U.S.); iii) Caribbean Cruise (approximate retail value $7,300 U.S.); iv) Hawaii (approximate retail value $ 9,550 U.S.); v) Greek Island Cruise in the Mediterranean (approximate retail value $12,250 U.S.); vi) France (approximate retail value $7,300 U.S.).

4. Any winner may choose to receive any trip or a cash alternative prize of $5,000.00 U.S. in lieu of the trip.

5. Odds of winning depend on number of entries received.

6. A random draw will be made by Nielsen Promotion Services, an independent judging organization on January 29, 1991, in Buffalo, N.Y., at 11:30 a.m. from all eligible entries received on or before the Contest Closing Date. Any Canadian entrants who are selected must correctly answer a time-limited, mathematical skill-testing question in order to win. Quebec residents may submit any litigation respecting the conduct and awarding of a prize in this contest to the Régie des loteries et courses du Quebec.

7. Full contest rules may be obtained by sending a stamped, self-addressed envelope to: "Passport to Romance Rules Request", P.O. Box 9998, Saint John, New Brunswick, E2L 4N4.

8. Payment of taxes other than air and hotel taxes is the sole responsibility of the winner.

9. Void where prohibited by law.